Confessions of a Side Dude
Disloyalty from the main chick

AUTHOR NAME

ISBN:978-1-7364746-0-0

DEDICATION

This book isn't really dedicated to anyone. I guess I can dedicate it to all the side dudes out there. Lol! Honestly though this book has a lot of factors from disloyalty, heart break, and pain. This is a way to show couples and people Lust isn't love and love isn't easy to maintain.

COVER MODELS
GUY: LAQUAN RANDOLPH
GIRL: ERICA MONROE

ACKNOWLEDGMENTS

I would like to say thank you to all the friends and family who took time to read and hopefully even buy the book. I also want to thank you the consumer for even taking the time to read this book. Even if you got it from a friend, I'm grateful. I want to give a special shout out to my daughter Shania. Your daddy is an author. For the last shout out, I want to thank my beautiful wife Ashya. I love you baby!

CHAPTER 1

HE DOESN'T HIT HOW I WANT IT

Clap, clap, clap, clap, clap. Mmm, Damn! This pussy is so good, Ryan says hitting it from the back while starring at Karah's fat, juicy, round ass. The sounds of her ass clap are like thunder on a stormy day. Whose pussy is this? Ryan yells out as he's gently and passionately stroking Karah's pussy. Mmm Karah moans trying to avoid an answer. Whose pussy is this Ryan groans as he gets closer to climaxing.

Karah still hesitant on giving Ryan an answer rolls her eyes in annoyance arches her back and throws her ass back and slams on Ryan's dick. "It's yours daddy", Karah says knowing that this gets Ryan to cum immediately.

Oooh God!! Ryan yells as he pulls out and shoots streams all over Karah's ass and back. Ah he screams as his man milk flies all over her. Damn baby, I love you! He yells at the top of his lungs. Unsatisfied and with a fake smile she replies, I love you too baby. Ryan in a daze stares at his marvelous paint job he gave to Karah. Um, hello! Karah says to Ryan to get him to snap out of his trance.

Sooo, are you just going to look and leave me like this? Karah asks. Oh, I'm so sorry babe let me get a towel Ryan says as he gets up and walks to the bathroom. His meat slapping his leg as he walks.

Make sure the towel is warm! Karah yells. Yeah yeah, I know, Ryan says running the water. Hurry up please. It's starting to dry up and you know I hate that, Karah says with an angry look on her face.

Damn girl relax, I'm coming. You already did that Karah says under her breath laughing to herself.

There you go all clean, Ryan says as he wiped away his seed from her ass. I'm going to go start the shower. Are you jumping in? Ryan asks. Yes, rolling her eyes. Just what I need more whack dick she says to herself as she meets Ryan in the shower.

On the other side of town Jamel is chilling with his homie Rashad playing the newest release of 2K. Damn nigga, you're trash! Jamel says as he scored a three.

Boy, you are only up by 5 points. So how am I trash? Plus, you use the best team in the game. If anything, you're the trash one Rashad says with a little frustration. Nigga shut up; Jamel says while laughing at Rashad. I can beat you with any team Jamel says while busting another 3. Well, put some money on it then Rashad says with a serious look on his face.

Ah you mad, Jamel says teasing Rashad. Nah, I'm just saying. You talk all that shit but never want to put any bread up. That's because every time you say put bread up and I beat you and you never want to pay up Jamel laughs. I'm dead serious! Rashad says while starring Jamel directly in the face. Put a stack up and let's see who wins! Rashad says so passionately.

I know you have the money and if you don't you can get it from that thick joint you've been smashing; we both know she's got it Rashad says while laughing.

Hahahaha!! Yea she got it he laughs. Side nigga of the year like shit Rashad laughs. Hey, it's the best deal. She's fine as fuck and that ass is just marvelous. I get all the benefits her man gets and all I have to do is fuck her. The jewelry, money, and trips all just off this dick.

Plus, I don't even have to be there emotionally. I'm living the life my nigga. Shit is good over here. If you had game like me, you would be living this life like me, but you wanted to go and get a girl Jamel laughs.

Yeah, you're living the life alright until that nigga finds out and fucks you up. Then it's all downhill from there Rashad says laughing uncontrollably.

That nigga doesn't want any smoke. I'll beat the shit out him. These hands are crazy Jamel says while throwing jabs and shadow boxing. Plus, it's not my fault that he can't fuck his girl better than me. That nigga needs to get his stroke game up. Lame ass nigga. I don't even know why she stays with that chump but it's still cool with me as long as he's there emotionally and I can keep fucking his bitch I'm great.
Aw shit! Rashad says looking down at his phone. What happened? Jamel asks. Man, my girl is calling. Rashad looks down at the phone hesitant to pick it up because he knows he's about to hear a mouth full.

Boy, you better pick that phone up with your scared ass. Last time she put you in time out for a month Jamel laughs.

Rashad picks up the phone. Hey baby, a ferocious but sexy voice lit up the phone. Nigga! don't hey baby me. Where the fuck are you supposed to be? Jasmin asked. Jasmin was a nice girl but feisty when pissed off.

Rashad sighs, are you deaf? I know you can hear me Jasmin barked in the the phone. I hear you man Rashad said in a low calm tone. Ok then so answer my question. Where the fuck are you supposed to be right now! Damn girl, why do you always have to call with that all energy? Rashad asks. You better have the same energy when you see me Rashad says in a tough tone.

Oh yeah, you're showing off. You must be around that dirty dick friend of yours Jamel. Yo! Why she bring me in this Jamel barks. She has no reason to bring me in it.

Chill nigga, she's just playing Rashad says laughing. No, I'm not! Jasmin screams through the phone. Nigga your dick is bound to fall off she laughs. Well, all 12 inches will hit the ground Jamel laughs. Eww! Nobody wants to hear about your nasty dick having ass Jasmin says in disgust. Yeah, whatever Jamel says laughing. So anyway, Rashad bring your ass you were supposed to be here an hour ago so we can get some food. I'm hungry so hurry your ass up Jasmin says. Before Rashad can respond Jasmin hangs up on him.

Ah, you in trouble Jamel laughs. Whatever nigga. I'll catch you later. Plus, a nigga is hungry Rashad says rubbing his stomach. Alright bet, you're lucky we didn't get to finish this game you would have taken a L.

Whatever nigga, we still betting that stack next time so be ready Rashad says as he walks out the door in a rush to get home to ease his impatient girlfriend.

See this is why I don't like chilling with niggas Jamel says shaking his head. Every time a nigga trying to bust a nigga ass in the game, they girl always call and ruins that shit. This is why I only like to fuck with bitches. Niggas always stuck up they girl's ass Jamel laughs to his self.

I haven't heard from Karah's ass in the last couple days. Let me see what she's up to. Jamel picks up his brand-new phone and texts Karah. "Hey boo" the message read with a smiley face emoji. This girl better text me back I need some of that pussy Jamel says laughing to himself.

The text message pops up on Karah's phone. Still in the shower Karah is not aware. Karah likes to leave her notifications on and visible for work purposes. It makes it easy for her to respond especially if it's an emergency or she can see who to ignore.

Damn, I forgot a towel Ryan says as he walks out of the shower. Turn the heat down too. That water is way too hot Ryan laughs. Shut up boy, there are two shower heads on each side feel free to use yours however you want instead of being all up on my side Karah says laughing. Besides it's not my fault your frail ass body can't take the heat Karah says while rubbing soap all on her body.

Ryan walking back from the closet with a towel on his arm walks past and notices Karah's phone is lit with a message.

Ryan picks up the phone. Usually this is no problem because they usually do this to each other since both of them live important lives. "Hey boo" Ryan reads the message with a confused look on his face. Ryan looks at the name and it reads Jamel. Ryan walks back into the bathroom still with that confusion on his face.

What's wrong with you Karah asks while turning off the water. Nothing you got a text message on your phone just now Ryan says in a calm tone. Ok, so what did it say? Was it important? Karah asks. Well, it's from a person named Jamel, Ryan pauses. Karah's heart starts pumping. Her mind starts racing. Oh god! I hope he didn't say anything crazy she says to herself. Karah knew she couldn't show any emotion on her face or it would tip Ryan off to her cheating, so she had to think quick.

Oh, Jamel, what did she say? So, Jamel is a girl Ryan asked. Yes, she's an old friend. We have known each other for years now Karah says calmly trying to avoid any indication of her nervousness.
I don't know any girls named Jamel Ryan says trying not to get aggravated. I know a few Karah says. Let me show you a picture. Karah pics up her phone and searches her social media page to find a picture of a girl she went to school with. See here she is. This is Jamel. Oh wow! She's really cute Ryan says laughing. Yeah, whatever Karah says a little aggravated. Aww, were you jealous? Karah mocks Ryan. A little Ryan said but I'm cool now. You know I would never cheat on you baby Karah says with a fake but confident smile. Yeah, I know but I don't know what got into me I'm sorry babe Ryan says with an embarrassed look on his face. It's ok baby Karah says while giving him a kiss.
Sooo, is there any chance of a threesome? Ryan asks. Boy bye, Karah says with a serious face. You know damn well I'm not eating any girl's pussy. You don't have to Ryan says while finishing getting dressed. We can just fuck her Ryan says laughing. Ok so you're trying to get slapped Karah says in a modest tone. See, you always get so upset Ryan says laughing. I was just joking you need to learn how to relax. Any way I have to go baby. I'll see you later I have a lot of work to do Ryan says bolting out the room and running down the stairs and through the door.

Damn that was close Karah laughs to herself putting her sexy black bra and panty set on. She picks up her phone takes a few sexy pictures and send them to Ryan along with a message that says, "I love you".

Karah looks at Jamel's message. "Hey boo", are you dumb? She responds. Jamel reads the message with a confused look on his face. Am I dumb? Jamel responds. Jamel's phone starts to ring. Hello, he answers with a ferocious tone seeing that it's Karah. First of all, don't answer the phone with all that attitude Karah says in an angry tone. You're the one talking to me crazy Jamel barks back. That's because your stupid ass almost got me caught up! Karah yells. Hold the fuck up! I didn't do shit! Don't blame me for your sloppiness Jamel screams back. Whatever, I told you to many times I will text you when I want some dick or when I need you for something. You're getting a little out of place, Karah yells back. So, all I am is dick and that's it? Wow! Alright I'll be that, Jamel laughs in a sarcastic manner. All you have ever been is good dick and that's it. You already knew what it was before we even started this shit so don't get brand new now. Alright you got it. You act like I want to wife your ass or something I was just seeing when's the next time we can fuck. Jamel laughs to ease the conversation.

Always jokes with you Jamel. This is serious you need to understand and get the big picture if you can't this shit is over Karah says in a calmer manner.

I got it man; Jamel says with a little bit of disappointment in his voice. I'll stay in my lane my bad Jamel says with a sigh. It's alright but to answer your question I need some dick ASAP Karah says laughing. Oh, see that's why you barking at me like that you need to cum a little bit Jamel laughs. No, I need to cum a lot Karah says holding her hand between her legs trying not to rub her pussy.

So then come over here so I can beat those cheeks Jamel says in a soft voice. Mmm, I would love to, but I can't Karah says with a sigh. Why not? Jamel asks. I just fucked Ryan and I wouldn't feel right if I fucked you right after. So, what, I know he didn't fuck you good and I know he can't fuck you as good as I can. If so, you wouldn't be wanting this dick right now Jamel says in a soft confident tone. I can't Jamel. That would make me feel awful and some type of hoe. So that's what would make you feel like a hoe and not fucking another nigga Jamel says under his breath. What did you say? Karah asks not hearing what Jamel said. Oh nothing, I was just saying to myself how bad I want that pussy. Don't worry soon I'll be bouncing all over that big dick Karah says with a slight moan. How soon are we talking? Jamal asks. Well, I was going to ask later but I have to go to Jamaica for this women's conference and I wanted to know if you would go with me Karah says with a shy polite voice. Why didn't you ask your man? Jamel asks. I don't want to go with him and I'm sure he will be busy anyway. Well, I'm down to go just let me know when we are leaving Jamel says with a smile on his face. We should be leaving next Friday and returning on Wednesday. Is that to close for you Karah asks. Nah, I should be good. I don't really have much to do. Plus, I can just get Rashad to run the shop while I'm gone. Alright cool Karah says cheesing ear to ear.

Since you're not coming over what are you doing? Jamel asks. Oh, nothing I just got out of the shower and I'm laying on the bed Karah says in a sexy tone. Oh word, so you're not going to put any lotion on? You're probably over there ashy as fuck Jamel says while laughing. You sure do know how to ruin a mood Karah says while laughing. I can also get that pussy juicy at any moment Jamel says with a soft serious tone. Mmm, how wet can you get me baby, Karah says while rubbing her breasts. I'll have you dripping just how you like it. Mmm, really Karah says while moaning. You got my pussy so wet right now. I want you to stroke that big dick for me while on the phone Karah says gently rubbing her pussy.

The phone rings and in Karah's ear. She looks and it's an incoming face time from Jamel. She accepts the face time and sees Jamel stroking his big hard shaft. Damn baby I love looking at you stroke your big dick as Karah looks in amazement. Show me how wet my dick makes you baby. Karah pulls her black lace panties to the side and shows her dripping wet pussy. Damn girl your about to make me bust Jamel says with a groan. I want you to cum for me baby. I want to see that nut shoot all over the place Karah says while moaning.

Kiss it for me Karah asks in a sexy voice. Jamel bends over and gives his dick a little kiss. Oh god! Karah screams as she's passionately fingers her pussy. I can't wait to suck your dick I need it in my mouth Karah moans. Mmm, yes, I can't wait to feel your tongue all over my dick Jamel groans. Jamel reaches over and grabs the oil sitting on the dresser.

He strokes his dick while applying the oil. His long thick shaft is glistening. Karah's mouth starts to water as she still can't help but think about having Jamel's shaft down her throat.

Jamel starts to spin his dick in a helicopter motion and smacks it on his thigh. The impact of the smack makes a loud thudding sound. I want you to cum for me Jamel says in a soft tone. Mmmm, baby I'm about to cum! Karah screams as she removes her fingers from her pussy and starts to rub her clit. Oh god! This feels so good baby. She spreads her legs and places the phone in a great angle so Jamel can see her juicy pussy. She starts to rub her clit faster and faster. I'm cumming baby! Her juices burst in the air and all over the bed leaving a huge puddle. She lays there still and panting. Her energy drained from her intense orgasm. Damn girl, that was sexy as fuck. I love seeing you squirt like that. That shit makes me want to cum. Karah picks up her phone and it's drenched in her juice. She rolls over and picks up a towel and whips it off. I want to see you shoot your cum, Karah says. Jamel starts to stroke faster, his balls start to tighten up, his thick hose starts to pulse. Ahhh! Shit! I'm cumming. Jamel's dick shoots load after load. His stream is thick and flies all over the place. Jamel's chest and hand are covered in his nut. Damn, that felt good he sighs. I wish I could taste it Karah says licking her lips. I can't wait to see you Jamel says. Same here baby, I need you ASAP. Alright well I'll talk to you later I need to clean myself up and shower Jamel laughs. Yeah, I need to clean up too. I made a huge mess Karah laughs. I saw, Jamel chuckles. See you later baby Karah says. Alright see you Jamel says. Karah blows him a kiss and the phone hangs up.

Chapter 2

Breaking the code

It's Tuesday a few days before Jamel goes on his trip with Karah. It's 9am and his phone starts to ring. Jamel looks at the phone his eyes hazy from being woken up out of his sleep. He looks at the name and it's Rashad. Jamel rolls over and hits ignore and continues to sleep.
A few hours later at about 12 in the afternoon Jamel starts to roll out of bed. He picks up his phone scrolls through social media and likes the pics of a few big booty girls that he's been eyeing. Damn! she's thick as fuck Jamel says with a grin. Her ass is stupid fat. I would kill her buns he says laughing. He goes to his text messages and see he has a message from Rashad that reads "Yo, I need a favor hit me back ASAP". Jamel decides to call Rashad to see what's going on. Rashad picks up the phone. Yo, what's up Jamel asks. Man, this girl is acting crazy Rashad says frustrated. Who? Jamel asks. Jasmin man Rashad sighs. Damn, what did she do now? Jamel asks laughing. She's talking about she needs some space and kicked me out. How she kick you out of a house that you help pay for and you're on the lease? Jamel laughs. That's what I'm saying but I'm a let her rock for a little I just need a place to stay for a little. Can I stay at your spot for a while? Rashad asks. Yeah, I got you bro Jamel says agreeing. Bet, she should be over to drop some of my stuff off Rashad says relieved. Ok bet, I'll be here. I'll wait for her Jamel says. Thank you, bro and Rashad, hangs up.

Later in the day Jamel is playing madden. He's playing online and is in a tough game with a very good player. The guy is not holding back and is talking shit in his ear every play through his headset. Damn, man you suck. The guy whose gamer tag is Tupe Fiasco says. Yeah, whatever Jamel says. You're getting lucky the game is cheating for you Jamel says in a serious tone. How come every time someone is getting their ass whopped it's "the game is cheating"? Tupe laughed. Jamel has the ball and it's the 4th quarter. The ball on the goal line it's 1st and goal. Jamel runs the ball with a stretch play, and it's stopped for a loss. You can't even score on the goal line, Tupe laughs hysterically. Jamel is silent and takes the slander. 2nd and goal, he tries to run again. He's stopped again. Try again Tupe laughs. 3rd and goal Jamel calls another run play. You better not try to run again Tupe laughs. You know better. Jamels face crunches up and his anger starts to burn. Jamel runs the ball, and the running back fumbles the ball and it's picked up behind the line. Hahahhahaha! I told you. You're trash dawg you can't even score bro. Go play FIFA or some shit Madden isn't for you. See this shit cheating for you again how the fuck did he fumble, and he hasn't fumbled all game Jamel screams through the microphone. It's 4th down Jamel doesn't have any timeouts. There is 20 seconds on the clock. He calls a pass play. He does a slant route with his number one receiver. The ball is picked off and Tupe runs it back and seals the game. Told you you're shit bro. Better luck next time he says and the game ends. Man, fuck this game Jamel says. I need to shower anyway. Jamel turns off the game and hops in the shower.

It's been an hour since Jamel has been in the shower. Jamel likes to take long showers as it helps relax him. He's standing in the mirror naked and didn't even hear the front door open. Ewwww, put some damn clothes on he hears. He turns around shocked to see Jasmin standing in the door. Damn girl, why the fuck do you just walking in peoples house? How did you even get in he asks in an angry tone? Don't act surprised. Rashad told me he told you I was coming Jasmin says sarcastically. Plus, he gave me a key. Damn, I forgot I gave that nigga a key a while back. All right take his shit in the spare room while I finish up Jamel says as he shuts the door.

Jamel is standing in the bathroom shaping up his hair. He finishes and looks around for a towel to wrap around to leave the bathroom. He looks and there aren't any towels around. Damn, I need a towel he sighs. He peeks out the door to see if Jasmin is around. He doesn't see her, so he runs to his room.
Jamel is putting lotion on his body not paying attention to the room. He starts with his chest and works his way down to his legs. He strolls back up and his body and starts to lotion his shaft. I thought I told you to put some clothes on? Jasmin starts laughing. What are you still doing here man? Jamel says with an agitated tone. I just finished putting Rashad's stuff in the room and was just telling you I was about to go and give you the key. You could have just left the key on the counter Jamel says. Well too late now Jasmin laughs. Oh alright, well leave the key and you can go Jamel says using a waving away motion. Jasmin stands at the door and looks Jamel up and down. She goes from head to toe and stops and his dick. She starts to stare. Damn, I didn't know you had it like that she laughs. Yo, why are you still here man? You got to go Jamel says with a straight face. I'm just admiring that beautiful dick she laughs. Can I touch it she says reaching out? No, Jamel says smacking her hand away. You are my homies girl how could I do that to him. He won't know because I won't tell. Plus, he's my bitch I got him on lock she says with a straight face. Don't disrespect my homie like that. Plus, he would know because I'm going to tell him. Well, do what you want but I'm going to feel that dick one way or another she says as she leaves the room and heads home.

Damn, women ain't shit Jamel says shaking his head. Should I even tell him Jamel says talking to his self. I will but I'll wait for the best time. I'm sure they will break up anyway. Plus, we didn't do shit and she was just talking crazy. Jamel's phone vibrates. Yo, did Jasmin bring my stuff over? Rashad asks. Yeah, she just left. Man, that girl is crazy Jamel laughs. Yeah, I know but that's my baby though Rashad laughs along with Jamel. All my shit is good right? Rashad asks with a serious tone. Man, I'm not going to lie she fucked those new Jordan's you got up Jamel says with a serious tone. What!!! I'm about to call this bitch. Why the fuck did she do that? Man, this is why we go through bull shit now. Jamel busts out laughing. I'm just playing dawg. All your shit is good. I was just joking. See you play to much Jamel. Rashad says in a serious tone. Yeah whatever, he says continuing to laugh. Yo, but I have to head to the shop I'll see you later Jamel says and hangs up the phone.

Jamel looks out the window and sees the sun is shining bright. He opens the front door just to make sure the weather is perfect. The weather app on his phone said it would be 80 degrees but feel like 95 due to the humidity. Bet it's nice as fuck I'm riding my bike today, he says. Grabs his helmet and goes to the garage and takes the cover off his motorcycle. He revs up the engine and just listens to the sound. His bike is all black Honda 600rr with a chrome spoiler. Damn I love this bike he says as he hops on and rides off.

After a long day at the shop Jamel decided to head home. Man, we need to start making more money he says to his self. He hops back on his Honda and since it's a nice day decides to head downtown to show off a little. He zooms in and out of traffic and pulls up next to a car with a few beautiful women. Yo, what's up? where are y'all going? Jamel says flipping up his vizor. We are heading to the mall the driver said turning down the music. The mall? Bet, how old are y'all. We are all 23. The passenger looks over. Do you have room for one more? She asks with a smile. Of course, I got a lot of room for you, Jamel laughs. Jamel unclips his spare helmet. She gets out the car, puts the helmet on and hops on the bike. You're just going to get on a motorcycle with a random? The girl on the back says. I'm grown I can do what I want the girl on the bike says in a smart tone. It's cool I don't bite Jamel laughs. You don't bite well maybe I should get off then the girl says laughing. Let me rephrase then. I only bite when needed he laughs. I make sure to never bite. I can open my mouth real wide the girl says in a jokingly but serious manner. Oh word, it's like that? Jamel asks. Yeah, it's like that. She says laughing. Well, I got a lot, so you better be ready he laughs. Hold tight he says and peels off.

They ride until the sun starts to set. Jamel pulls up to the scenic view. He parks the bike, and they get off. We have been riding all this time and I never got your name Jamel says with a smile. Aiyana is my name. What's yours? It's Jamel he reaches out his hand for a handshake Aiyana reaches back. Nice to meet you Jamel says laughing. Same to you Aiyana says laughing back. Don't get upset for what I'm about to ask you but what are you? What do you mean? Aiyana asks with a puzzled look. Are you asking what my ethnicity is? Yes, like where were you born and all that. Well, I'm Indian, Aiyana says. Bet, salute to all the Indians out there. The white man did you dirty killing off your people and all that. No! I'm Indian not Native-American. Aiyana has a frustrated look on her face. My bad queen no disrespect. I can be culturally clueless at times. It's ok, you wouldn't be the first person to say that she laughs to ease the tension. Also, I was born here in the United States which some people also find it hard to believe. My parents immigrated here before I was born and bam here I am. Jamel looks her up and down. Aiyana is a very beautiful girl, with long black hair and Hazel eyes. She's not the type of girl Jamel would usually go for since he has a slim body and small breasts and barely any ass, but Jamel sees something he really likes in her. Why are you staring at me? Aiyana asks. No reason you're just so beautiful and I want to get to know you more. Plus, I still want to see how wide that mouth opens Jamel laughs. Alright I'm cool with that but it's getting late and I have to get home Aiyana says. They hop back on the bike; Aiyana tells Jamel a place close to her house but not the exact address just in case he is a creeper.

Jamel pulls up. It was nice meeting you; Jamel says. Same to you, Aiyana replied. Cool, as Jamel is about to pull off. So, you're not going to get my number? Aiyana looks puzzled. Damn, I'm sorry Jamel laughs. I just thought since you gave me an address away from your house you weren't interested. Aiyana looks confused. How did you know that? We are at the end of the street on the curb, he laughed. True, she replied. Jamel pulls out his phone and give it to Aiyana. She puts her number in. I'll text you later he says to let you know it's me. Alright cool, Aiyana says with a smile. Jamel pulls off and heads back home.

Jamel pulls up to his house. He parks his bike and heads up the stairs and opens the door. He sits on the couch and turns on the TV. It's 11 at night and Jamel turns on the Lakers game. Damn, Aiyana is fine as hell, Jamel says to his self. He walks to the back to see if Rashad is there. Jamel knocks on the door. Yo Rashad, are you up? He doesn't hear anything and peels through the door to see if he's there. He opens the door and sees Rashad laying there sleep and also to his surprise he sees Jasmin laying there in almost nothing. Oh shit! He says as he shuts the door lightly and heads back to the living room.

He continues to watch the game. Damn, what the fuck type of shot was that? He yells at the tv. Man, I hate how the offense flows. Damn ref! Where's the foul? He yells. Why do you have to be so loud? Jamel turns his head and sees Jasmin standing in the hallway. She is barely covered in anything but in her all black bra and panties. Damn! Jamel says to his self as he looks Jasmin up and down. Jasmin is a beautiful girl, with 36 DD breasts, long black hair, and brown skin. She's on the short side with being 5'2 but her height and body works perfectly with her 125-pound frame. Jamel is mesmerized by her beauty. Her red lip stick pops on her skin tone. Jasmin sometimes where's a nose ring Jamel always thought it looked good on her but never wanted to tell her because he didn't want to gas her up or overstep his boundaries. Jamel gets up and walks to the kitchen. He gets some chips out of the cabinet. Jasmin walks in the kitchen and opens the fridge. Her ass is poking out. Jasmin doesn't have a huge ass but man it's perfect and a great bubble shape. Jamel snaps out of his trance from her beauty. Yo, go put some clothes on. You're being mad disrespectful right now. Jamel continues to look her up and down. You know you like what you're seeing right now, Jasmin says with a smirk. No, I don't, and my homie is in the back sleep you're really out here like this while your man is back there. That's messed up. Don't worry about him Jasmin laughs. I know you like my body you can't keep your eyes off of it. Yeah, whatever Jamel says with a straight face. So, you don't like these. Jasmin pulls down her bra and her big breasts bounce out. Jamel starts to get erect and he can't control it as he stares at her big areola's. Jamel has a slight fetish for them and seeing hers makes him super excited. Jamel turns his head away. No, I don't like those. Once again, you're my homies girl and I would do him foul like that. Didn't I tell you not to worry about him? Jasmin says with a smile. She walks over to Jamel moves out the way and heads back to the living room and sits on the couch to finish the game.

Why are you being so difficult? Jasmin asks Jamel rolling her eyes. I'm being loyal and a friend unlike some people. Jamel says starring at the tv trying to avoid eye contact. You know you want me Jasmin says moving to the couch. She eases over to a spot right next to Jamel. I can see your dick is getting hard she says laughing. Jamel stays silent. She reaches over and grabs his stiff man hood. Yo, what are you doing? Don't touch me. You keep saying one thing, but your dick is saying another Jasmin smiles. Jasmin takes Jamel's hand and places it between her legs in her panties so he can feel how wet and how juicy her pussy is. Hmmmm, I know you feel how wet you got me. You can't tell me you don't want this. Jasmin whispers in his ear. She takes his fingers off her pussy and sucks his fingers tasting her juice. Damn, I taste good she says still whispering in his ear. Jamel can't hold on any longer and wants to give in to her. Baby! Where are you at, he hears. Rashad is awake and looks for Jasmin. She gets up puts her bra back on and heads back to the room. Jamel is relieved and decided to head to his room and go to sleep just in case she decided to come back. Hopefully she's gone and never comes back. Now I have to go to sleep with this hard ass dick he says shaking his head. He heads back to the room and goes to sleep.

The next morning Jamel is enjoying his sleep. He's lying there and then he feels a warm sensation on his dick. Slurp, slurp, cough, slurp. This sensation feels wonderful he can't help but enjoy. Am I dreaming? He says to his self. His dick starts to pulse. Give me that cum he hears. Jamel opens up his eyes and sees it's Jasmin sucking his dick. Aye, what are you? Jamel can't even finish his sentence her head is too good. Oh shit, I'm about to bust Jamel says. Jasmin looks Jamel directly in the eye. She starts off slow and places all of Jamel's man hood in her mouth and deep in her throat. She flicks her tongue on his balls and that sends him over the edge. Jamel grabs her head and leaves it there. Oh shit! oh shit! Jamel's dick starts to pulse, his balls tighten up, and he shoots his load deep in Jasmin's throat. Jasmin swallows his seed without any hesitation and keep Jamel's dick in her mouth until it goes soft. She gets up, smiled and left the room and headed out the front door. Jamel is confused as to what just happened. Damn, I can't believe this bitch but damn her head was fire though. I see why Rashad is with her. I have to tell him though I can't do him like that. Jamel gets up puts some basketball shorts on and heads to Rashad's room. He knocks and the door opens. The room is empty all Rashad's stuff is gone. I wonder if he found out what happened Jamel said to his self. He picks up his phone and texts Rashad. "Yo, what's good. You alright? I see all your stuff is gone". Jamel waits for a response. Damn, I hope he's not tight man it wasn't my fault.

CHAPTER 3

Off to JAMAICA

It's Saturday and Jamel still hasn't heard from Rashad. Shit, he must be tight. My nigga hasn't hit me up in a few days. Man fuck that bitch! He says packing up his stuff. He texts Karah. Are you coming to get me? Karah picks up her phone and looks with a smile. I can't but I'll order you an Uber. She sends with a smiley face. Ok cool, Jamel responds.

What are you smiling at? Ryan asks looking at Karah. Oh, nothing. I'm just ready for my trip. I'm sorry I can't make it. Ryan says gently touching Karah's chin. It's alright, I know you're busy. She says with a fake smile. Alright, let's go you're about to be late and miss your flight. Karah and Ryan head out the front door and head to the car. On the other side of town Jamel's Uber is out front he puts his stuff in the car and heads to the airport. After 15-minute ride Karah arrives at the airport. She looks around to see if she can see Jamel. She doesn't see him and is happy to avoid any conflicts or explaining. Do you need help with your bags? Ryan asks with a smile. No, I'm fine. Thank you though. Alright, I love you. I love you too. Karah walks in the airport and Ryan pulls off.

Karah had went through checking her bag, getting a little bite to eat, and boarded the plane and still no Jamel. He better not be standing me up she says with an angry tone. Last call for flight 3557 to Jamaica. Hello passengers, my name is John I will be your Captain for this flight. The weather is looking good at about 80 degrees and sunny. Please remember to fasten your seatbelts as we are good to go once the door closes. Karah starts to get more frustrated. She picks up her phone to send Jamel a nasty message. Excuse me ma'am. Can you please put your phone up? We are about to take off she hears. I will put it up when I feel like it! She says with base in her voice and looks up to see it's Jamel. See, you play too much. She says laughing. Why do you look so tight? Jamel laughs. You were about to get your ass cussed out Karah laughs. My bad I got caught up in traffic, but I'm here now so relax. Whatever! Karah says rolling her eyes. They buckle their seatbelts, the flight attendants make their announcements, and the plane takes off.

Jamel and Karah has been on the flight for an hour and a half. Karah looks over at Jamel. He's been sleeping for the last half hour. Jamel wake up. Karah says shaking Jamel's shoulder. Jamel opens his eyes and looks at Karah and went back to sleep. Wake up I said. Karah lightly smacks Jamel in the face. Yo, what's your problem? All I'm trying to do is sleep. I haven't seen you in weeks and we have all this time, and you want to sleep. Karah says with a slight attitude. Man, we have almost a week you need to chill. Jamel says starring at Karah. I'm a chill alright. Karah presses the button and the flight attend comes. Do you need something ma'am? The flight attendant asks with a smile. Yes, may I please have a blanket I'm a little cold and want you to take a nap. Jamel looks over and shakes his head at Karah. The flight attendant walks away and comes back with a blue blanket. Here you go ma'am. Do you need anything else? No, that's all. Thank you so much Karah says with a smile. So, you asked for a blanket to sleep when you just gave me some shit for sleeping. Jamel says with a little bass in his voice. Oh, I don't need it to sleep she says with a smile. Jamel has a confused look on his face. Karah places the blanket over their bodies. She reaches over and grabs Jamel's dick and takes it out of his pants. Damn, I missed this big dick, she says stroking his dick. Show me how much Jamel says with a smile. Karah gets underneath the blanket and starts to kiss Jamel's dick slow. His dick starts to harden. She slowly starts to lick the base of his shaft. She bends over and her face is in his lap. She starts to suck his dick taking him deep in her throat. Damn, I missed this head Jamel says softly. Karah starts to move her head up and down holding the base of Jamel's shaft. The excitement of possibly getting caught puts Jamel over the edge. I'm about to cum. Karah takes Jamel's dick out of her mouth and starts to stroke it. Oh shit! Jamel shoots his load all over Karah's hand. Karah gets up and heads to the bathroom to clean her hands. She comes back to see Jamel with a smile on his face. Jamel and Karah head back to sleep for the remainder of the flight.

Jamel and Karah got their bags and headed to a hotel via a cab. Let me ask you a question Jamel says looking at Karah. Sure, what's up? Karah responds with a smile. How come you never let me nut in your mouth? I don't like the taste of cum. Plus it's gross. No, it's not. That shit is sexy as fuck Jamel laughs. I agree, the cab driver says looking through the mirror. Who asked you? Karah says in a direct tone. My nigga, Jamel says laughing. The cab ride is silent for the remainder of the trip. After about 30 minutes the driver pulls up to the hotel. That will be $30 please the driver says with a smile. Karah reaches in her purse and hands him a $50. Keep the change she says getting out the car. Jamel and Karah walk into the hotel. Karah goes to check in and gets the key. We are in room 512 Karah says handing Jamel a key. They head up the elevator and head into the room. They place their bags on the ground and both plop on the bed and head to sleep for the remainder of the day due to an exhausting flight.

It's morning and Karah gets out of bed. She moves lightly to not wake Jamel. She strips down to get in the shower. Karah stops at the mirror. Damn, I need to lose some weight I'm starting to get big. Karah grips her ass and rubs her stomach. Jamel looks up at Karah. What are you talking about? You're fine as fuck. Jamel moves behind Karah and grabs her belly. I need all of this he says with a smile. Thank you, Karah says with a smile. I can tell I'm getting too thick though Karah replies. Girl ain't no such thing as too thick Jamel laughs. Plus, I love the way you look. Jamel starts to move his hands all around Karah's body. He stops at her pussy and places his hands in between her legs. Karah lets out a slight moan. See, I can't be messing with you I have to get ready and go speak today. Can I go? Jamel asks with a smile. No, everyone from work will be there and I don't need any distractions. Alright, I'll just lay around and chill then. Karah hops in the shower. She stays in for about 15 minutes to avoid being late. She lotions up and puts on her black blazer and fitted dress pants. How do I look? She asks starring at Jamel. Amazing! He says in excitement. Ok, I'm off Karah walks out the door and leaves Jamel alone on the room.

Jamel decides to get dressed and heads downstairs to get some breakfast. Damn, I'm hungry as shit! We didn't even eat dinner last night. Jamel starts to rub his stomach. He patiently waits in line to get his food. Jamel grabs 2 pancakes, 5 sausage links, 4 strips of bacon, and an orange. He sits down at a table by himself in the corner. The room is pretty full and there really isn't any place to sit.
Jamel is in the middle of his delicious meal when a beautiful lady walks in. Jamel can't help but stare. She looks at Jamel and smiles. Jamel smiles back. She walks over, is it ok if I sit here? She asks with a smile. Of course, you can. Jamel gets up and pulls her chair out for her. How nice of you. She says with a smile. My name is Keisha. Nice to meet you Keisha I'm Jamel. What brings you to Jamaica Jamel asks? I'm here for the conference. I was supposed to speak today but they rescheduled me for tomorrow. How about you? Keisha asks. Well, I'm just here supporting a friend. It was a free trip and so I said why not. What are you doing after breakfast? Keisha asks. I really don't know what to do. Jamel's sighs. You should come with me there is a party at a beach that starts in a little and lasts all day. I'm down, Jamel says with a smile. Great my cab is outside. Jamel and Keisha finish their food, go downstairs to the cab, and head to the beach.

Keisha and Jamel arrive at the beach. I forgot I don't have a towel or anything. It's ok, I have two. Plus, we don't really need anything at all at this beach Keisha says laughing. What do you mean? Jamel asks with a puzzled look on his face. Oh, you'll see. Keisha smiles at Jamel as they arrive at the beach.

Jamel holds Keisha's bag for her they get to a sign that reads "no clothes beyond this point". What type of beach is this? Jamel is confused to what's going on. Keisha ignores Jamel and starts to strip. Jamel can't help but stare at her body. Keisha is a fine, slim thick woman. She has beautiful chocolate skin. Damn you're fine as fuck. Jamel says in awe of her beauty. Thank you, I try my best she laughs. Jamel looks her up and down. He stops at her pussy. What's wrong? Keisha asks. Is my hair a problem? Or is it my labia? I love hair on pussy it makes me feel like I'm with a grown woman. Keisha is a little self-conscious about being fully nude due to her hating the way her vagina looks. Her labia hangs out and is kind of long. I love all that shit Jamel says with a smile. Keisha smiles, thank you. Some men don't know how to take it and showing it makes me feel uneasy that's why I wanted to come here. So, I can try get over it. You just happened to be a consultation prize. Keisha starts to laugh. I believe it's your turn. Jamel looks down. I'm not sure if I'm ready. My dick isn't the biggest and I'm nervous. It's ok, I won't judge Keisha smiles. Jamel starts with his shirt, he then removes his shorts, he turns around and holds his dick so Keisha can't see. Are you ready? Yes, I'm ready. Jamel turns around. He lets go of his dick and it bounces up and down. Oh my god! Keisha's eyes open wide. Damn, you have a big dick. Jamel's dick is slightly erect from starring at Keisha's body. I knew I made the right choice Keisha laughs. Ok let's go. Jamel and Keisha walk to the beach.

At the conference Karah is a little bored. She doesn't mind speaking because she feels it can help women be the best version of themselves. They are on break, so she decided to call Ryan. The phone rings and Ryan picks up. Hey baby, how's the trip? Ryan asks. It's alright, kind of boring. We are on a break now. What are you doing? Karah asks. Nothing just finishing up some work. That's good, maybe when you get back to the room, we can have FaceTime sex? I don't know I'm probably going to be tired Karah yawns. I understand, well enjoy I'll talk to you later. Alright, I love you. Ryan hangs up the phone. Damn he's rude he didn't even say I love you back. Karah calls Jamel but doesn't answer. Oh, so now he can't answer my calls alright I'll get his ass later. Karah heads back to finish up the conference.

Jamel and Keisha are enjoying their day in the nude. They stop and admire the beautiful bodies and occasional couples having sex on the beach. The warm weather and beautiful water make for a great day. They sit and enjoy some jerk chicken and rice and peas from a vendor who's trying to make a living. This chicken is good Jamel says barely taking the time to chew his food. Yes, it is but you should show down I'm sure he has more. Keisha starts to laugh and pokes fun of Jamel. It's getting late so maybe we should head back. That's fine with me but first you know what I never done before? Keisha starts to smile. What's that? Jamel asks. Have sex on the beach. Keisha looks Jamel up and down and can't help but think about his dick inside her. We just met are you cool with that. Jamel wants to make sure she's alright with what's about to happen. Oh yes! Keisha responds quickly. I don't have a condom though. Are you clean? Keisha asks Jamel. Yes, I get tested every few months. Alright me too. Just pull out alright. Yeah, I got you. Jamel starts to smile his dick starts to rise in excitement. Let's find a good spot. Keisha walks Jamel over to a nearby spot behind some rocks. She pushes Jamel against the rocks and starts to rub his dick. Jamel bends her over and leans down to taste her. He licks her pussy and noticed her big clit. Damn, you have a big clit. Is that a problem? Keisha turns away in embarrassment. Hell no, lay on your back. Jamel is excited. He leans in and starts to suck on Keisha's juicy clit. She moans and tells him to keep going. He swirls his tongue all over her pussy. Keisha grabs Jamel's head and pushes him down. I'm about to cum! Keisha let's out a loud moan and cums all over Jamel's face. Jamel's face is covered in her juice. He smiles and takes the towel from Keisha's bag and whips his face. Mmmm, you taste good. Jamel rolls Keisha over and grips her ass. He smacks her ass and watches the sand brush off and her ass bounce. Jamel slowly inserts his hard shaft inside Keisha. Keisha stops him halfway. I can't take all of it please only go this far. I got you. Jamel slowly strokes her pussy. His strokes get faster and faster. He avoids going to deep at the request of Keisha. Damn! I never had a dick this big before, she says in excitement. She clinches her pussy tight on Jamel's dick. Go a little deeper I want to see if I can take it. Jamel agrees and goes deeper. Slowing his stroke down. Oh god! Keisha screams. I'm going to cum! Cum on this dick baby! Jamel grabs Keisha's hips. He strokes faster. Fuck! I'm about to cum too! Don't stop, cum with me! Keisha says without any hesitation. Jamel can't hold it back any longer. He lost control and slammed all of his dick in Keisha. Oh fuck! They both scream. Jamel groans and shoots a big stream of cum in Keisha. Jamel realizes he went too far. Oh shit! I'm sorry I went to deep and I came in you. It's alright, it was worth it Keisha smiles. The cab should be here now. Keisha and Jamel head to the cab and take a trip back to the hotel.

Keisha and Jamel arrive back at the hotel. It was nice meeting you Jamel says smiling ear to ear. Nice to meet you too Keisha says with a grin. Hopefully I'll see you around. Jamel and Keisha walk off and head to their rooms. Jamel opens the door to the room. Karah is up reading a book. Where have you been? Why are you covered in sand? I was at the beach Jamel says walking to the bathroom. How was the conference? Well, if you would have answered my calls you would know. Karah stares at Jamel in anger. I'm sorry I was out having fun. Yeah ok, Karah says turning her head. Are you going to give me some of that dick? I had a long day. Not tonight I'm tired. Jamel hops in the shower. To wash away the sand and sex. He gets out and Karah and Jamel fall asleep.

It's 6am and Karah is up getting ready. She looks at Jamel sleeping and can't help but smile. Why couldn't I meet you first she says to herself. Karah heads out the door to go get some breakfast.

While eating her food Karah looks and sees her best friend and coworker. Hey boo! Karah yells to get her attention. Hey girl! How was speaking yesterday? It was boring but good. What happened to you yesterday? Karah asks with a smirk. Nothing much they canceled me yesterday, so I went on a little trip and had me a hoe moment. A hoe moment? Karah looks with a smile. I need to know all about this. Well, I met this fine ass dude yesterday we went to a nude beach, and long story short I fucked him. You fucked him! You just met him. Don't judge me Karah. I couldn't help it. If you would have seen his dick you would understand. He ate my pussy and fucked the shit out of me. Did he wear a condom at least? No, but it's cool I'm on the pill. He may have a disease. Girl, you have to be more careful. Karah shakes her head. I'll get checked when we get back, he assured me he was clean. Alright I need to meet this man. Karah laughs while finishing her food. Did you get his name? Yes, his name was Jamel. Jamel? Karah's faces starts to scrunch up. Her blood starts to boil. What's wrong? Are you ok? Yes, I'm fine. Karah is pissed but doesn't want to let her friend see. Alright, I'll see you later I need to go. Alright see you Keisha. Keisha walks off and leaves Karah to sit all alone and deal with her feelings.

Karah heads up stairs and is furious. She bursts open the door. Jamel jumps up. What's your problem? Jamel looks with a confused look on his face. You're my problem! Karah screams. What did I do? Jamel is confused he's not sure what's going on. You have the nerve to fuck another bitch when I brought you here. Jamel's face shifts he's confused to how she found out. Yeah, I fucking caught you I can't believe you would do this to me. Karah sits on the bed her eyes blood shot red. Jamel stands up. I think you need to remember your place! Jamel yells.

CHAPTER 4

Worst trip ever

What the fuck did you just say to me! Know my place! You really got me fucked up. Karah balls up her fist. You don't like how that shit sounds do you? How's that shit feel? I'm not your man. We just fuck! All I am is dick remember so don't come at with me this bullshit. Jamel looks at Karah's hands. You better un ball those fists because if you swing, I'm equal opportunity when it comes to ass whippings. Karah un balls her hand. She calms down a little. Look you need to get out. I can't have you stay in this room with me.

Bet, I'm good. I don't need to deal with this shit. Plus, I fucked your friend so I'm good. Jamel gathers his items and heads out the room.

Karah sits on the bed and gathers her thoughts. She realizes that she has to speak again soon and heads to the conference.

Karah walks backstage. Hi, Ms. Jones. The backstage assistant says with a smile. Apparently, we have something special for you so can you hold right here for a moment please? Sure, but what is it? Karah says confused. Well, I can't tell you, but I will say it may brighten up your day. The assistant walks off. Karah sits down on a chair. The assistant comes back a few minutes later holding what looks like to be a note or a letter. Alright, Ms. Jones we are ready for you now. Karah gets up, walks on stage and sits in her chair.

Jamel is sitting in the lobby. Damn, I can't believe this bitch! How's she going to talk about how I need to stay in my place but she's catching feelings and acting like I'm her man. I guess I kinda get it though but at the same time she needs to feel where I'm coming from. I didn't know the girl was her friend and if I did, I wouldn't have fucked her. Damn, maybe I should go apologize. Excuse me sir. Yes, can I help you? Jamel looks up and noticed it's a hotel staff manager. Are you ok? You're over here talking to yourself. Are you staying at this hotel? Yo! I think you need to mind your business. Jamel stands up and looks the man in the eye with a death stare. Well guests here are my business sir. You looked a little out of it and giving all that's going on I want to make sure my guests and staff are safe. If you can kindly show me your room key I will be on my way. Bitch! I'm not some crazy bombing up shit dude. What the fuck do I look like? Fuck you! Fuck this hotel! Fuck Jamaica! I'm leaving soon anyway. I think you need to leave before I call the police sir. The manger points to the door. Fuck the police! I'm not scared of the fucking police! I got some shit to do and then I'll leave. Jamel walks off to head to the room where the conference is. The manager walks behind him to watch what he's doing. Sir only speakers and people with passes are allowed in. Jamel looks back at the manager. Why are you following me? I said I have business. Jamel opens the door and sees Karah on stage. Karah notices Jamel and the manager behind him. She sees security coming in after Jamel. Excuse me for a second. Karah walks off stage and heads to the door from around back.

Hi, what's going on here? Karah looks at Jamel in disgust. Do you know him Ms. Jones? The manager asks with a smile. Yes, I do. What's the issue? Karah is trying to avoid eye contact with Jamel. The sight of him makes her stomach turn. Ok, well this gentleman is being asked to leave. We just wanted to confirm that he was staying here. Is he staying with you? Karah pauses, she wants to say no, but her heart won't let her. During her moment of silence, the backstage assistant walks up. Hi, Um Ms. Jones I don't mean to interrupt but we need you back on stage. I'm sorry give me one moment please Karah says talking to the manager. Karah walks away with the assistant and heads back on stage.

Welcome back Ms. Jones the host of the event says with a huge smile. So, we have a special surprise for you. Music starts to play. Karah is listening she notices it's her and Ryan's song Promise by Jagged Edge. She looks around confused. Karah picks up her microphone. Wow! This song has a special place in my heart. This is the song that was playing when I first met the guy, I'm in a relationship with. We play it every now and then and he sings it to me. The verse starts the lights cut off. Karah hears a voice.

A spotlight brightens up and it goes to a person leaning down in the back row. The man has a low hat and black coat. Karah is trying to figure out what is going on. The man starts to sing with the song.

Karah starts to get embarrassed. She starts to recognize the voice. The man walks in the center aisle. He's walking at a steady pace to get to the front of the stage. The song stops. The man takes off his hat. Karah is smiling ear to ear. Ryan? What are you doing here? Ryan drops to one knee. Oh my gosh! Karah screams in excitement. He takes off his coat and reveals his shirt. The shirt is a white tee with a picture of Karah and Ryan on their 1st date. Under the picture the words read will you marry me. The backstage assistant walks down to Ryan and hands him the card she has been holding. Karah, I love you. You are the best thing to ever happen to me. I can't picture my life without you. I wrote a poem for you. Ryan picks up the card and begins to read it. "The 1st time I saw her face I didn't know it was destined to be but when we met again, I knew it was for real. The love I feel was that of a new mother to her child. I couldn't stop thinking about you. My dreams and my imagination spread through the galaxy's hoping one day my heart would meet yours. As my heart burned for you only your soul could put out the flame. The goddess of my life, the soul to my body. My tears became yours. My hands your own. With that we built a foundation of love. I will always remember what it is to be in love. My air is pouring with your breath. A love so deep, my queen of the earth you are my everything I will always remember your love". The crowd of women starts to cheer. Ryan places the card down. Karah jones, will you do the honor of being my wife.

The crowd is silent waiting for a response. The silence is broken by a loud scream. What the fuck! Jamel screams in disbelief. Karah looks up she waves her hand to signal she wants Jamel removed from the hotel. Ok sir it's time to go. Security grabs Jamel by the arm and starts to push him down the hall. I'm so sorry about that Ms. Jones. The hotel manager says sympathetic to the current situation. It's ok, can't anyone especially a man ruin this moment for me. The answer is yes. I will marry you. The crowd starts to cheer. The satisfaction of watching Jamel get manhandled by security and watching her get engaged was a great feeling. Karah walks to the front of the stage and jumps off into Ryan's arms. They kiss passionately and her a loud aww from the crowd. Karah can't wait to get Ryan back in the room so she can give him Ryan the best head and sex he has ever gotten. The excitement has her pussy flowing.

Outside the hotel Jamel is sitting there on the curb. The police arrive. What seems to be the problem the officer says. He's slightly aggressive towards Jamel. Nothing man, Jamel says with an attitude. Who are you talking to like that boy? Jamel can tell this officer isn't here just for casual conversation to get to the bottom of the issue. The manager jumps in as he sees the tension. Hey officer, we had a slight issue, but everything is alright now. Well, I think we still have an issue here the officer says getting in the face of Jamel. Do we still have an issue boy? No sir, no issue at all Jamel says looking down. That's what I thought. The cop bumps Jamel and gets back in the car. Jamel looks over at the manager. Look man, my bad. I was just going through some shit. I'm leaving now though. Sir, I get it. Stuff happens but that officer is no good. It could have all been bad for you. Especially with him. I've seen it personally he's not one you want to deal with especially in a place you're not from. I understand, thank you man. Jamel sticks out his hand and the manger sticks out his and they shake hands.

Karah and Ryan are at the door to her room. So, what was that about at the door. That guy looked crazy. It sucks that our moment was ruined by that loser. Ryan says laughing. I'm sure he's not a bad guy Karah says with a smile. Do you know him? No, but he may be having a bad day. Don't judge a book by its cover baby but enough with all of that I'm still happy and he didn't ruin anything. So, let's go in and celebrate. Karah grabs Ryan's hand and tries to open the door. My key card won't work. What the hell is going on?
Ryan and Karah head to the elevator. I paid all this money to stay here and my shit doesn't even work, Karah says with an attitude. She folds her arms and starts pacing waiting for the elevator. Relax it's not that big of a deal, Ryan says laughing. Yes, it is that big of a deal. They are fucking with my flow. I had some plans for you, but they fucked it up. The elevator finally comes. Karah storms in. Press one please, Karah says in a demanding tone. Ryan ignores her and presses floor forty. Ryan, I said press one. What the hell are you doing? Karah is pissed. Ryan ignores her. Ryan, I know you fucking hear me! Damn, relax girl. Ryan says with a smile he can barely hold in his surprise. The elevator moves at a good pace. Karah is getting more impatient. We can just get off on the next floor and go down, Karah says with frustration. The door opens on the next floor Karah tries to get out, but Ryan presses the button, and the door closes in her face. Ryan! What the fuck! Karah is really upset. Why are you playing games? Ryan ignores Karah. He holds the floor and the door closed button so the elevator will go straight up to the floor without stopping. The elevator stops at floor forty.

The reason why your card doesn't work is because I upgraded our room. The door opens. Ryan and Karah walk to the door. Ryan takes the card key and slides it into the door. The door opens and Karah's eyes light up. The room is really big and beautiful. Wait here, Ryan says as he walks off. I can't believe he did all of this, Karah says to herself. To think I was going to throw all of this away for some dumb ass nigga who can't even get a business started. Ryan walks back in the room with a blindfold. Put this on. Ryan hand Karah the blind fold. Don't peak either. I won't peak, Karah says laughing. Ryan moves behind Karah to check to make sure the blindfold is adjusted tight to make sure Karah can't see. Ryan grabs Karah's hand and leads her to the bedroom. The smell of vanilla candles lights up the room. Lay down and put your hands behind your head. Ryan what are you doing? Did I say you can speak? Ryan says in a serious tone. Now shut up and lay down. Yes daddy, Karah says in excitement. Ryan takes Karah's hands and handcuffs her to the bed. Karah is surprised. Ryan has never been like this. Ryan takes some massaging oil and rubs it all over Karah's body. The oil has a warming sensation. Ryan un cuffs her and makes her turn over. He re handcuffs Karah while she's on her stomach. Ryan jumps off the bed and heads to the bathroom. Karah still can't see what's going on due to her blindfold. A few moments later Ryan comes back in silk boxer briefs and oil on his body. Put that ass in the air, Ryan says with authority. Karah doesn't hesitate. She gets into doggy position. Ryan pulls out a whip and smacks Karah in the ass. What the fuck? Karah screams. Didn't I say shut up; Ryan says with authority. Karah's pussy starts to drip. She's never been whipped before and it has always been a fantasy of hers. Ryan whips her again even harder. Karah lets out a big moan. Oh! Yes, daddy I've been a bad girl. Spank me daddy! Ryan pulls down his pants and pulls out his dick. He gently starts to ease in Karah's pussy. Karah's pussy clinches on to his dick. He starts to stroke faster smacking her ass with his hand. Fuck this pussy baby! Ryan has never made Karah feel this way and she's excited. Ryan pulls out. He goes to head back in. He acts like he's going for her pussy and slides right in her ass. What the fuck! Ryan, I don't like anal! Ryan ignores her. He strokes harder. He gets as deep in her ass as he can. At first it hurt but Karah is starting to enjoy it. Fuck my ass daddy! Ryan moves out her ass and shoves his dick back in her pussy. Oh god! I'm going to cum! Karah screams. Ryan sticks a finger in Karah's ass, and she

Squirts all over the bed. Ryan gets up and heads to the bathroom to get some towels. He un cuffs Karah and to his surprise. She's fast asleep. Ryan places the towels underneath her body to soak up the wetness and heads to sleep beside her.

Jamel is in the cab headed to the airport. He managed to get the airline to transfer his flight to today free of charge by sweet taking the customer service women on the phone. What happened to the beautiful lady you had with you before? Jamel didn't notice but it was the same cab driver they had on the way to the hotel. I had to head back on some business but she's still there. Did you enjoy your stay? For the most part. I did have some fun. I would love to come back here soon; Jamel says with a smile. The cab driver pulls up to the airport. Thanks for the ride, Jamel says with a smile. Anytime you're in Jamaica and you need a ride let me know. The driver hands Jamel a business card with his phone number on it. Thanks bro, I'll keep you in mind when I come back. How much do I owe you? It's $40 flat but if you have any pictures of that sexy lady from the other day to show me then I'll take $10. Ok bet, Jamel scrolls through his text messages from Karah. He finds one with her in the mirror laying on her stomach with her ass in the air. Here you go bro. The cab drivers' eyes start to light up. Damn! She has a fat ass. You've been hurting that? I was used to but not anymore, Jamel says laughing. Don't even worry about the money this ride is on me. Thanks, Jamel says and walks into the airport to check in.

Jamel heads to the kiosk. The machine says there is an error, so he heads to the line to speak with an airline associate. He hands the clerk his passport and boarding pass. Hello Mr. Smith, the clerk says with a smile. I tried to check in, but the machine won't let me, so I had to come over here. Give me one second please. Hmm, well Mr. Smith. Your flight has been cancelled. What do you mean cancelled? Jamel's face starts to twist in anger. Well, per my system it says that there is an issue with the plane, and it won't be able to take off today. Aw man, so when's the next available flight? Well, we can get you on one tomorrow. For this issue we are willing to give you a flight voucher that will pay for your food, hotel, and bump you up to 1st class. That sounds great! Instead of the money being used to a hotel can I just have it for a future flight? I don't really need a hotel. I can just wait here until the flight is ready. Well, if you were past the gate and through TSA then that would have been fine but since you're not TSA won't let you through the gate without the proper paperwork. Alight cool, I guess there's really nothing I can do about it now, so I'll just take the deal. The airline associate hands Jamel his vouchers for the select restaurants and hotel. Give me one moment Mr. Smith, the airline associate walks away, and a manager comes over. Hello sir, thank you so much for your patience with us, the manager says extending his hand for a handshake. It's alright, I really wanted to go home though man. I'm kinda disappointed in your airline for something like this happening. I don't know if I want to travel using your airline again. Jamel fakes that he is super disappointed to see what else he can milk out of the manager. I totally understand sir. I see you are a Diamond member, and we can't have this happening so here's $600 to go with your vouchers. Jamel didn't correct the manager due to it is Karah who booked the flights and see if the diamond manager, but he took the money and vouchers and left the airport to head to the hotel. It's late after Jamel checked in, he headed upstairs and went to sleep.

Karah wakes up to an empty bed. She looks around but doesn't see Ryan. Ryan walks out the bathroom brushing his teeth. Good morning, Ryan says with a smile. Good morning, Karah says smiling back. Last night was crazy, Karah says with a grin. Yeah, I know, Ryan says back smiling ear to ear. I have to go back home so are you staying here? Ryan has to finish his big project. No, I'll head home too. I'm done here plus I don't have to speak anymore so I'm good. Karah gets out of the bed still naked. Damn! You gained some weight baby. That's not something you say to your future wife Ryan, Karah says with an attitude. I'm sorry but I'm just being honest. Well keep it to yourself. Karah starts packing their stuff to head to the airport.

On the other side of town Jamel wakes up and starts packing. Damn, this was still a dope trip. I can't wait to go back home though. Jamel calls a cab and heads to the bathroom to brush his teeth. He's packed and ready to go. He heads to the cab and on to the airport.

Karah and Ryan are dressed and ready to hit the airport. A cab picks them up and they are on their way. To Karah's surprise it's the driver that picked her and Jamel up when they first arrived. Nice to see you again, the driver says with a smile. Nice to see you too, Karah smiles. Do you know him? Ryan asks. Yes, he picked me up before when I first arrived. Oh cool, Ryan says looking down at his phone. The cab pulls up to the airport. How much do I owe you? Oh, it's a free ride. It's pre-paid for. Really? By who Karah asks. The gentleman before paid. What gentleman? Ryan is confused. Probably just someone trying to pay it forward, Karah says to keep Ryan from noticing what's going on. Ryan gets out the car. The man showed me you and your body is nice. If anytime you're back look me up. The cab driver hands Karah a card. She throws it down in disgust and heads into the airport with Ryan.

Kara and Ryan board the plane. While there she is surprised by who she saw. Jamel is sitting in the seat right across from theirs. Karah is in a panic. Jamel looks up and shakes his head while laughing. Karah doesn't know what to do or say. Jamel is a prime side nigga, so he still knows how to play his role. He looks up smiles and puts his headphones on and goes to sleep.

Karah is still on edge. Ryan looks over. Man, he looks familiar, he says holding his chin. Probably just mistaken identity, Karah says quick on her feet. Maybe you're right. Ryan places his headphones on as well and heads to sleep too. The 6-hour ride seemed like forever.

CHAPTER 5

Cuck what?

It's been a few weeks since Jamel returned, and he hasn't heard from Karah. After he arrival of the plane Karah looked at Jamel and mouthed thank you and ever since he respected what was going on. On the other hand, he still hasn't heard from his boy Rashad.

Jamel is sitting in the living room when he hears a knock at the door. Who is it? It's me open the door. Jamel opens the door and sees it's Rashad. Damn nigga! What's up you dodging me or some shit? I've been hitting you for a minute now. Oh shit! Yeah, my bad. Remember I told you I was going out the country too. I was in Africa and ended up in the fucking jungle and didn't have any service. Then I dropped my phone in the fucking water. I had to wait to get back to get another. Damn son, I forgot. I was like I hope my nigga isn't upset with me or some shit. Why would I be upset? Rashad asks with a confused look on his face. Well because you're girl. My girl? What she do?

Jamel pauses, at that moment there's a knock on the door. Hold on one second bro. Jamel walks over and opens the door and Jasmin busts through the door. Hey baby, Jasmin says to Rashad. Hey, Rashad says back with a smile. What's going on? Jasmin asks seeing the disgust in Jamel's eyes. Jamel was just telling me you did something and was about to tell me, so I want to know what you did. Oh, that's nothing. Jasmin turns around and smiles at Jamel. I'm sure he liked it; she laughs. My nigga your girl sucked my dick! She did what? Rashad has an angry look on his face. You're supposed to be my nigga! How can you do that man? It wasn't my fault bro. She's a hoe. She tried to get me the fuck her I said no. Oh, so you decided to get some head instead! Rashad starts to raise his voice.

The room is silent again. I'm sorry my nigga. It's fucked up I should have told you. You're sorry! Fuck your sorry! Rashad starts to walk toward Jamel. Yo, you're my boy but at the same time if you swing it will be on and popping in this bitch, Jamel starts to put his hands up to prepare for the potential scuffle.

Rashad and Jasmin burst out laughing. Jamel looks confused. What the fuck is so funny? I'm telling you how this bitch cheated on you and you're laughing! Ok, first thing stop calling my girl a bitch. Second thing is I already know. Jamel scrunches his face up. What do you mean you already know? Jasmin and I have a special relationship. What kind of special relationship? You just go around and let her suck your friends dick? Kinda, you were the next step. She has never done this with a friend you're the first one. It kinda was a test run. My nigga! I'm not understanding shit you're saying right now. Ok, Jasmin and I have a cuckold relationship. Cuck what? Jamel looks more confused. To keep it simple I like to watch or listen to Jasmin be with other people. So, you let her fuck other dudes? Yes, I let her fuck other guys. I actually like it. She sends me videos and sometimes I'm even there when she does it. Do you get to fuck other women? Jamel asks to try and understand the situation better. I asked if he would, Jasmin interrupts but he says he doesn't want to. Jamel's face looks shocked. You don't fuck other bitches my nigga? Nah bro, I thought about it, but I love the cuck lifestyle. We have done threesomes with girls, but I just like watching another man fucking my girl. It's the disrespect and the fact that she's just being a slut to make me happy it gets me excited. Yo, to each their own bro. You should have told me so I wouldn't have been tripping on her that hard. Some people don't know how to take it that's why I didn't say anything to you about it. I didn't want you judging me and shit, Rashad says looking down. You're my homie, we are damn near brothers and known each other forever I wouldn't judge you and I never will. Jamel walks over to Rashad and daps him up. Thanks for telling me too that makes me feel even better knowing you're really my best friend. That's one reason why I wanted to try it with you. It kinda sucks you didn't go through with it though. Rashad and Jasmin both start to laugh. Hey, no disrespect but it was hard not to. Jasmin is fine as hell. How was her head though? Rashad starts to smile. Her head was fire I almost busted instantly and thought it was a dream. I know my mouth game is like that, Jasmin starts to laugh. How about we give Jamel something special for being such a good friend, Jasmin says with a smirk to Rashad. That's a good idea as long as he's ok with it, Rashad smirks back.

Man, I don't know, Jamel says with an unsure look on his face. This shit is a lot and kinda weird for real. It's only weird if you think of it that way. Plus, if at any time you want to stop, we are all for it, Rashad tries to ease Jamel's feelings. Are there any rules that I should know? Jamel wants to make sure he doesn't do anything to disrespect his friend or his girl. Well, just don't cum in her hair. Rashad and Jasmin start to laugh. I'm just ready to feel that big dick inside me, Jasmin says as she bites her lip.

Look, if y'all are into it then I'm down. I haven't had some pussy in a minute, and I need some ASAP, Jamel says laughing... That's all I needed to hear; Jasmin says walking to Jamel. She pushes Jamel on the couch and pulls off her shirt. Her big breasts bounce in her red lace bra. Jamel starts to pull down his pants. Oh no you don't have to do that baby I got you, Jasmin says in a sexy tone. She gets on her knees and pulls Jamel's pants down and takes them off for him. She stares at the big bulge in his briefs. It looks like you are already warmed up, Jasmin smiles. I told you it's been a minute, Jamel laughs. Rashad stares in excitement. Fuck the shit out of him baby! Show him how much of a slut you can be. Rashad can't help but get excited. Watching his girl service his best friend is a dream come true for him. Jasmin pulls off Jamel's boxer briefs. His dick springs up to attention.

Damn bro! no wonder why she wanted to fuck you so bad your dick big as fuck, Rashad says in amazement. Yo, I'm down with this but you got to chill on that gay shit, Jamel says with a straight face. I'm sorry bro but I'm just saying. You're blessed man. Sit there and shut up! Jasmin says taking control. You know better than to talk this much unless I give you permission, Jasmin says to Rashad with a straight face. Yes ma'am, I'm sorry. Jasmin picks up Jamel's dick and holds it with two hands. Mmmm, your dick looks so tasty. I loved the taste of your cum last time. It's so long and thick. I need this to stretch me out now. Jasmin starts to jerk Jamel's dick using both hands. She twists her wrists in a circular motion and sucks the tip at the same time. Damn, you sucking the shit out my dick already. Jasmin moves her hands and goes deep on Jamel's dick taking him deep in her throat. She doesn't gag and keeps bopping up and down. Swirling her tongue around his shaft. Jasmin takes Jamel's dick out of her mouth. She jerks him off with one hand and kisses the tip of his dick. Jasmin looks directly in Jamel's eyes. She holds the base of his dick and sucks and jerks him at the same time. Jasmin deep throats Jamel's dick again and again. Covering his dick in spit. God damn! No wonder why you got her bro. Her head is crazy. Rashad doesn't respond to Jamel he's silent. The excitement of his women pleasuring his best friend is intense for him. Jasmin takes Jamel deep in her throat again. Oh fuck! Jamel can't hold back. Jasmin notices Jamel's dick starts to tighten up. She holds the base to prepare for his tasty seed. Jamel arches up a little. Jasmin moves her hand and sticks a finger in Jamel's ass. Oh shit! Oh shit! Jamel shoots 6 long streams of cum down Jasmin's throat. Jasmin holds some cum in her mouth moves from inside Jamel's lap and walks over to Rashad. Jasmine looks at Rashad and opens her mouth to show him the prize she was just awarded. Good girl, Rashad says with a big smile. Jasmine swallows the rest Jamel's cum and kisses Rashad in the mouth. Taste that niggas nut you cuck bitch! She says with passion. Rashad starts to jerk his dick from the passionate kiss. You don't have my permission to cum yet, Jasmin says with authority. She walks over to Jamel. That was quick I thought we would get to fuck I'm kinda disappointed. I need that dick in me baby, but I guess maybe another time.

Jamel snaps out of his trance. He walks over to Jasmin grabs her by the arm and takes her to the bedroom. Rashad follows behind. Bitch! You got me fucked up. You think a nigga is done? Get on the bed and spread those cheeks. Jasmin eyes light up. Her pussy starts to drip due to the excitement. Jasmin loves when other men talk to her like that and makes her feel like a slut.

Jamel stands behind Jasmin. He places his hand on her back while the other hand holds his dick to guide it into her pussy. Jamel's slowly starts to insert his dick into Jasmin's pussy. Jasmin starts to moan. Mmmm, it's so big. I don't know if I can take all of it, she says. Oh, you about to learn today, Jamel says with a straight face. Jamel sticks his dick in her again this time going a little deeper. Oh shit! It's so big! Jamel pulls his dick out and slaps it on her ass. Jamel slips his dick back in Jasmin's pussy. He goes as deep as he can using all of his 12-inch goodness to break her walls. Oh my god! It's so big I don't know if I can take it all. You can take it baby; Rashad says cheering his girl on. Yo, Rashad come over here. If she wants to be treated like a slut, you need to help her.

Rashad walks over to Jamel and Jasmin. Jamel sticks his dick back in Jasmin. Now Rashad I need you to help her bounce on my dick, so she won't be running and shit. I want you to see how a real nigga fucks your bitch. Spread her cheeks and watch how deep a nigga get in her pussy. Rashad obeys Jamel's command without any hesitation. He spreads Jasmin's ass cheeks apart and watches while she takes Jamel's dick. Good my nigga. Now while her ass is spread make her bounce on my shit. Rashad doesn't hesitate as he's spreading her ass for his best friend, he starts to lightly push Jasmin all the way on his dick. Oh shit! Jasmin screams out. This feels so good. I feel it so deep inside me. Jasmin looks up at Rashad. You like watching your girl be a slut for you, don't you? How does it feel helping your girl get fucked by such a big beautiful dick? Mmm, help me baby. Help me bounce on this monster dick, she says in enjoyment. I'm about to cum! Jasmin screams out. Cum on his dick. You have me hard as fuck right now, Rashad says while grabbing his dick. Jasmin's pussy starts to cream from her orgasm. Look how much your girl loves my dick bro, Jamel says smirking. She creaming all on my shit. Jamel starts stroking Jasmin long and hard. Rashad's assistance helps him get deeper inside of her.

Rashad looks at Jasmin's face. The view of pleasure on her face is sending him over the edge. Baby, I need to cum now. Jamel interrupts don't ask her for shit. She's our slut right now. We do whatever we want while I'm fucking her. Isn't that right Jasmin? Yes baby, do whatever you want to me. Just don't stop fucking me. See bro, your girl said it we can do whatever you want to her. I say we split roast her. Rashad pulls out his dick and it's caged. This is on my dick she makes me wear it; Rashad says with an embarrassing look on his face. Take that shit off man. Rashad goes into Jasmin's purse and gets the key. He unlocks his self and his 3-inch dick springs up.

Rashad walks back over to Jasmin and Jamel. Jamel pauses for a moment. Rashad you hit it from the back while I get some of that fire head. Jamel moves and lets Rashad take his place. Rashad easily enters Jasmin's stretched pussy. Damn, you really stretched her out my nigga. Rashad is happy being inside his girls destroyed pussy. Rashad starts to stroke faster and faster. That's right baby fuck my stretched pussy. I can barely feel your small dick inside me. Rashad gets more excited. Hearing Jasmin make fun of his dick size it gets him even more turned on. Jamel smacks Jasmin in the face with his dick. Don't worry about him you need to clean this dick off. Jasmin looks in Jamel's eyes and wastes no time taking him deep in her mouth. That's right suck all your cum off my dick. Jasmin takes Jamel's 12 inches again with no problem. It amazes Jamel how she can swallow all of his dick when most girls he's been with can barely swallow half of it. Mmm, my cum tastes so good, Jasmin says with a smile smacking Jamel's dick on her lips. Jamel pulls his dick away from her mouth. He walks next to Rashad. I think she's ready bro. Ready for what? Rashad looks confused to what Jamel is talking about.

Jamel whispers in Rashad's ear. Rashad gets a big grin on his face. He stops fucking Jasmin and moves out of the way. Jamel lays on the bed next to Jasmin. I want you to ride my dick, Jamel says to Jasmin. Jasmin springs up and jumps in Jamel's lap. She grabs Jamel's dick and glides it in her pussy. Jasmin starts to bounce up and down. She starts of slow and picks up the pace. Jamel waves Rashad over. Jamel holds Jasmin close to his body and takes control. Jamel starts pounding her pussy. Jamel stops stroking her. Rashad positions his self to enter Jasmin's ass.

Rashad bends over and spits on his dick. He slowly tries to glide into Jasmin's ass. Oh my god! Jasmin screams with enjoyment. Jasmin has never been double penetrated by two men, but it has always been a fantasy of hers.

Jamel looks Jasmin in the eye. Bounce baby, he says I'm a soft tone. Jasmin starts to bounce taking both dicks at once. She moves faster and faster. Rashad places his hand on her back to stop her from moving and takes control. He starts to pump harder. Jasmin clinches her ass tight on her man's dick. Fuck my ass baby! This feels so good. Fuck my slutty ass baby! I'm about to cum again. Fuck my ass harder! Rashad pounds Jasmin's ass harder and harder. Fuck! Fuck! Fuck! I'm cumming. Jasmin's body starts to convulse from her intense orgasm. She never had an orgasm like that before.

Jamel is trying to hold on but can't anymore. Fuck! I'm about to cum too! Where do you want me to cum? Cum deep in my pussy. I want your seed deep inside me. Jamel grunts, he starts to pump her faster. Jamel shoots spurts inside of Jasmin's pussy. Jasmin starts to move her pussy deeper on Jamel's dick taking all of his kids deep inside her. Rashad takes his dick out of Jasmin's ass. Jasmin rolls off of Jamel's body huffing and puffing. Spread your legs, Rashad says to Jasmin. She spreads her legs and opens wide for Rashad. Rashad places his face in her pussy. Rashad starts to eats Jasmin's pussy. He starts by slowly licking her clit. He then licks all around the lips of her pussy. Jasmin's starts to push out Jamel's cum. Rashad watches as his best friends cum oozes out of his girlfriend's pussy. He licks his lips and eats her pussy tasting Jamel's cum. Jamel looks over in shock. He doesn't say anything because he doesn't want to ruin the moment. Rashad starts to beat his meat while he continues to eat her pussy. Jasmin takes Rashad's head and pushes him closer to her pussy. Eat my pussy, make sure to clean your slut's pussy, Jasmin says palming Rashad's head. I'm about to cum, Rashad says stroking his dick. While still stroking his dick, he gets up and places his self over Jasmin's body. Rashad strokes his dick faster and faster. Ahhhh! Shit! Rashaad shoots streams of cum all over Jasmin's breasts and face. Jasmin takes her hand and rubs his cum all over her body.

Rashad looks over and Jamel is knocked out cold. Damn baby, I think you drained him, Rashad says laughing. You know that's what I do, Jasmin snickers. Do you think he will mind if I use his shower? No, I shower here all the time. Plus, he just let lose in you so it's the least he can do, Rashad laughs.

Jasmin walks over to the bathroom and jumps in the shower. Rashad pulls some clothes from a bag they brought in the house. He joins Jasmin in the shower. Thank you baby, Rashad says lightly touching Jasmin's face. You're welcome, she says with a smile. Jasmin and Rashad wash each other sensually cleaning every inch of their bodies. So, did you like it? Rashad asks Jasmin. I loved it! I was scared at first, but it worked out great. I'm glad you liked it hopefully we can do it again. Can I fuck him by myself? Well after this I would really like to be there. I don't know how I would feel about it now if I wasn't there to watch. I understand, Jasmin says. They get out of the shower and head to the guest room and head to sleep.

The next day Jamel wakes up to the smell of bacon and fresh fruit. He looks down and he's still naked with his leg covered in cum and Jasmin's juices. He gets up and puts some basketball shorts on and heads to the kitchen. He sees Jasmin cooking and Rashad sitting at the table. Good morning bro, Rashad says. Good morning, Jamel responds. Last night was crazy, Jamel laughs. Yeah, it was Rashad laughs. Jasmin walks over and hands her two men a big plate of food. Eat up my handsome men, she says with a smile.

Jamel starts to eat his food. I got to ask you man. What made you get into that? Jamel asks. Well, as you saw last night, I have what's considered a micro penis. I used to be embarrassed by it. You know a lot of men also have this issue that they deal with penis size. Jasmin was the first who embraced my small penis which gave me confidence. We sat down and talked about it and then we chose this lifestyle. Now doing this and shaming my penis makes me excited and happy. That's what's up man. It's good to embrace what and who you are. I used to have a small dick when I was younger then bam one day my shit grew crazy. Thanks for picking me though, Jamel daps up Rashad.

Jamel, Rashad, and Jasmin finish their meals and get ready for the day. Jasmin cleans up for Jamel and her and Rashad head home. Jamel walks back to his room and heads back to sleep. Jamel sleeps and dreams about the great night he has before and hopes it happens again sometime soon.

CHAPTER 6

Life of Ryan-Why did he really purpose?

It's been about a month since Ryan proposed to Karah. Ryan for a while was doing better in making sure he was available for Karah and spending time with her. That was really short lived due to Ryan's busy schedule. The question is what made Ryan really propose?

Beep, beep, beep, beep. It's 5am and Ryan wakes up to his alarm going off. He reaches over and hits the button to turn it off. Ryan lays there for a second looking up into the sky. I wonder if I made a mistake, he says to himself. I do love Karah, but I don't know if I was really ready to be married. Plus, I'm extremely busy lately. Ryan looks over at Karah sleeping peacefully. A smile braces across his face. Nah, I made the right choice. Well at least I hope I did.

Ryan rolls out of bed. He walks over to the bathroom and turns on the shower. He didn't notice that he turned the water all the way to blazing heat. Ryan jumps right in without even testing the water to see if the temperature is right and the perfect way, he wants it. Fuck! That shit is hot. Ryan hurried up and jumped back out of the shower. His body in pain from the heat. He reaches in the shower and turns the heat down. Ryan takes his toe and tests the water to make sure it's fine this time. All right, that's better. I can't believe I did that stupid shit. Well, at least that woke me up this morning. After a 15-minute wash Ryan hops out the shower. He brushes his teeth and rinses his mouth with mouth wash. All fresh and clean, he says while breathing in his hand to smell his minty breath. Ryan walks in the closet and takes out his light grey suit. He goes for the drawer and picks out a pink dress shirt. Yeah, I'm a kill em today, Ryan laughs to himself. Ryan irons his clothes, gets dressed and heads to work.

Ryan is sitting at the light. The light just turns green and he proceeds to go. The person in the car behind starts to honk their horn. The car starts ridding real close to Ryan's bumper. Ryan throws his hands up and motions the driver to drive around him. The young couple in the next car switch lanes next to Ryan and puts the window down. Ryan puts his window down and looks over. Learn how to fucking drive! You're slow as fuck! People have places to be, the driver says in an angry tone. Ryan stays calm. Calm down the light had just turned green. Wherever you have to be I'm sure it's not that important I'm sure you will be alright. Fuck you! You're about to make me late. I made you late? Take responsibility for your own actions. Ryan puts up his window and drives a little faster to avoid the altercation. The driver zooms past Ryan and cuts him off. The driver hits his brakes to try and get Ryan to re end them. What the fuck! Ryan yells. The lady in the passenger seat sticks her middle finger out the window and throws a cup of coffee out the window and it splashed all over Ryan's windshield. The black Mercedes speeds off leaving Ryan pissed off.
Ryan heads to the car wash before he heads back on his way to work. He picks up his phone and calls his assistant. Thank you for calling The truth gaming, office off Ryan Clark. How can I assist you today? Hey Erika, it's Ryan. Oh, hey Mr. Clark. I must have missed you when you came in do you need me to get you something? Oh no, I'm not there yet. Some asshole tried to run me off the road and threw coffee at my car. Oh lord! Are you ok? Yes, I'm fine. I should be there in about 15-20 minutes. Ok great, I'll let the two people you have scheduled to meet with know. Oh shit! I forgot I had two interviews set up for today. Tell them I'm sorry and I'll be there as soon as I can. Sure thing, Mr. Clark. See you soon. Erika hangs up and Ryan proceeds to head back on the road.

As Ryan pulls up, he notices a Black Mercedes is parked in his assigned parking space. Ryan is calm headed so he decided just to park somewhere else and will ask Erika to move it later. Ryan walks in the office. Hey, Mr. Clark I have the two potential candidates waiting for you in the conference room. Cool, but hey who's Mercedes is that in my spot? Oh, I believe it belongs to the gentleman who came into interview. The two people you have scheduled today must know each other since they drove in together. After the interview can you please move my car for me? Ryan asks with a smile. Anything for you Mr. Clark, Erika says with a wink. Ryan really likes Erika. He ended up hiring her despite the negativity it brings in his household. She's a nice girl but Karah doesn't like her. Karah doesn't like the fact that he's spending all of his time with such a beautiful girl. Erika is a white woman. She's about 5'5 with long blonde hair. Erika is what Ryan likes the call the new breed of white women because she is thick in all the right places and the white women he has met before were not.

Ryan walks into the conference room looking down at the resumes he printed out. I apologize for being late I had a few issues this morning please forgive me. The young man speaks up. Don't worry about it. I understand how it is. Your voice sounds really familiar. Ryan looks up and to his amazement it's couple from this morning. Don't I know you two? Ryan asks. The man looks puzzled. No, I don't think we have met before. The woman says the same. Maybe just a mistaken identity Ryan tries to play it off. So, let's start the interview. I will be interviewing you both together is that alright. Yes, that's fine they both agree. Alright cool this will give me a chance to see how you both do with answering questions while others are around. It also helps me get both done at once. It's more like whoever has the best interview wins kinda thing. Alright, first question for you sir. Tell me about a time when a person was getting aggressive with you. How did you handle it? What was the outcome? Well, I'm not an aggressive person, the man says with a smile. I stay calm and collected at all times and try to pick the best outcome and calculate the situation. The man pauses waiting for Ryan's response. That's interesting, Ryan says with a smirk. You didn't answer the question for me though. I asked to describe a time for me and how would you handle it. For example, earlier today I was driving here. A car was behind me at the light. The car driver was aggressive towards me and almost ran me off the road. Also, the passenger threw coffee at my car. How I handled it is I was upset at first, but I calmed down and didn't let it affect my day. Do you have a similar situation like that? Ryan asks. The woman's eyes light up. Oh my god! You're the man from earlier this morning. What guy? The man asks. The one you cut off. I told you about driving crazy like that. Yes, that was me, Ryan says with a straight face. This job I was really looking for people who show patience and are not hot heads. You two didn't show the qualities of the people we are looking for here. The woman starts to frown. To be honest I don't even know this guy like that. We just met through mutual friends and just happened to have the same interview. I didn't want to even throw the coffee he made me. Did he also make you stick up the middle finger at me? The women are silent. Here I also like to hire people who don't throw others under the bus when they feel the heat. So, I guess we are not getting hired? The man asks. Nope not while I'm here at least. Fine I didn't want to work for such a pussy anyway! The man starts to get loud. Well John, I'm pretty well known in this industry in this area so good luck. John walks out the room. The woman pauses and meets Ryan at the door. If I fuck you can I get the job? Ryan holds up his hand and places his ring in her face. The woman storms out the room.

The remainder of the day is relaxed for Ryan. He's in and out of meetings all day and has to work late again. It's late at night and Ryan is just getting home. He walks in the room and turns on the light. Karah roles over. Turn that off I'm trying to sleep. I want to tell you about my day it was crazy, Ryan says excited. I don't want to hear it right now I'm tired Ryan. I'll listen tomorrow. Ryan is disappointed Karah doesn't want to hear what happened to him. He undresses and heads to sleep for the next day.

Ryan decides to head to work extra early to get started on his huge workload. It's 4am and he walks into the building. The room is silent and dark. Ryan flicks on the lights in the building. He walks to his office and opens the door. Oh shit! I'm so sorry he says. He sees Erika standing there half naked in a black band tee and some boy shorts. Her ass can barely even fit in her underwear. Oh my god! This is so embarrassing. I was hoping I would get up before you even got here. Did you sleep here last night? Yes, I did and I'm so sorry. I didn't have anywhere else to go Erika starts to cry. Is everything ok at home, Ryan is really concerned. Well you know I have been with the same person for a year or so. At first everything was fine but then there was a death, then came heavy drinking, now here I am sleeping at work hoping not to get fired, Erika starts to sob. Don't worry I wouldn't fire you. You're the best assistant I ever had. Yeah right, if it wasn't for this ass I would have been gone, Erika starts to laugh. I mean the ass helps but I'm serious you do a great job. You can stay here as many times as you need just let me know a head of time. How about this you go to the locker room, shower up, change and we can get some breakfast. Does that sound good? Yes, that sounds great. Thank you so much Ryan this means a lot. You're welcome, Ryan smiles. Erika heads out the door and to the locker room to change and prepare for the day.

After a nice breakfast Ryan and Erika head back to the office. While in his office working Erika knocks on the door. Hey Ryan, Mrs. Holmes is here to meet with you. Shit! I don't want to meet with her is there any way you can tell her I'm not here? Uh, I kinda already said you were in here working and I would check to see if you're busy, I'm sorry. It's ok, it's not your fault Erika send her in. Well, hello Ryan, she says as she walks in the room and lightly closes the door. Hello Kathy, what brings you by today? Well I came to check on things to see how my money is being spent. Everything is right on time and we are crushing the deadline, Ryan smiles. Great, well another reason why I'm here is I've been texting you, but it seems like you're ignoring me what's going on with that. Nothing, I've just been extremely busy, Ryan lies. Also, good, Kathy walks over to Ryan. I wouldn't want you or that good dick to be upset with me at all. Kathy grabs Ryan's dick. Erika burst through the door. Hey Mr. Clark, I forgot to schedule this, but you have an important call like right now. Erika is surprised by what she saw. Oh my! I'm sorry to burst in and interrupt. It's ok sweetheart. I was just leaving. Kathy walks out the door and smiles on her way out.

While on his business call Ryan is freaking about what Erika saw earlier. He can barely even pay attention to what the meeting is about. The call lasted for about an hour. His day is close to being done. After the long call Ryan walks out of his office. Uh Erika, can you come into my office please. Sure, Erika says with a smile. Look I want to talk about what you saw or possibly heard earlier. I didn't hear anything Mr. Good dick, Erika starts burst out laughing. So, you were listening? I heard a little bit of it. I mean that woman is kinda loud. Ryan puts his head down in shame. Look, whatever you have going in your personal life is your business. I won't say a thing I mean who cares if you fucked her. Well, your fiancé might but other than that that's your business and I'm not to get into your personal business. I was just shocked because I didn't think you would do that to Karah. Well, let me explain what happened.

It was the night before Karah was to speak at her conference. Ryan was working late night with Kathy. Man, we got done a lot today, Ryan says yawning. Yes, we did. I'm happy all this is going great and working out, Kathy replied. Would you like to call it a night then, Ryan suggested? I got a better idea since we worked so hard how about we get a drink, Kathy smiles. Eh, I don't know about that. I don't drink that much and I'm kinda of tired, Ryan responds. It will be fun, and drinks are on me. Are you really going to turn down an offer from a pretty lady? Kathy bats her eyelashes. Yes, yes, I am, Ryan laughs. Well, as your financial backer this an order, Kathy laughs. Fine I will go but only one drink. Great, I'll drive. Kathy grabs her purse and keys and heads out the front door to her brand-new Audi R8. Holy shit! This is your car? Well, it's my loser husbands but what's mine is his so I guess you can say its mine, Kathy starts to laugh. Man, this is my dream car. Really? I never really cared for it. You're crazy this is like what a $200,000-300,000 car. Yes, but that's really nothing. We have way more expansive cars than that. He and I actually don't want it anymore, but no one seems to want to take it she laughs. Well, I would love to drive this thing. Here you go. Kathy tosses Ryan the keys. Really? Are you sure about this? Yes, go ahead. Drive to your hearts content. Aw, man thanks. This is like a dream come true. Ryan hops in the driver's seat and starts the car. He sits in shock for a little. Alright, we will go to my favorite place Kathy says. Just follow the GPS. Yes ma'am, Ryan says as he pulls out of the parking lot and heads to the bar.

After about a 30-minute drive they pull up to what appears to be an abandoned building. Ok let's go inside. I'm not sure about this Kathy. Trust me everything will be fine. Ryan and Kathy walk to the door. She knocks 2 times. The person on the other side knocks back once and the door opens. Can I help you? A voice whispers through the crack of the door. We are here for the open house, Kathy responds. Open house? Ryan has a confused look on his face. The door opens all the way and a big man opens the door. The man stood about 6'7 and weighed about 325 all muscle. The man looked intimidating then a huge smile ran across his face. Hey Kat, he says excited. Hey Nick, she responds while reaching for a hug. The bouncer looks over at Ryan. Is he cool? Yeah, he's cool. He's a first timer he won't tell what's going on here. Alright cool, the man moves to the side and opens the next door and to Ryan's amazement it was filled with what had to be hundreds of people.

At first the night was normal then there was a sudden change. As the night went on the people upstairs slowly started to disappear. It seems like everyone is done partying maybe we should head out, Ryan says sipping his drink. Already, then we would miss the good part, Kathy laughs. Good part? Ryan looks confused. Suddenly the room goes completely dark. The DJ changes the music to soft late-night R&B. The crowd of people suddenly start to re appear this time with different outfits. Kathy, what the hell did you bring me to? These people disappear and come back naked and if they are not naked, they barely have anything on. This is a secret club for the elite of this town. It's a good way for you to meet new people. Plus explore a little. Is this a sex club? Ryan is very confused. I guess you could say that. Oh man I have to get out of here I'm in a committed relationship I can't be here. Look Ryan there is a reason why I brought you here. I want you. I know you can tell. Kathy, that's nice and all but I'm with Karah. Can we go please? No, I want to stay and have fun. I specifically want to have fun with you. I'm sorry that can't happen, Ryan says shaking his head no. It's going to happen. I don't get told no. When I want something, I get it. You have a choice to make either you fuck me, or you say bye to your game because I will pull out of backing you for this game. Ryan looks shocked. He can't believe what he is hearing. Ryan heart is torn. He loves Karah but he worked so hard to make his dream come true. So, what will it be? Kathy looks Ryan in the eye with a straight face. Alright, I'll do it. That's what I want to hear Kathy grabs Ryan's hand and leads him downstairs.
Walking down the stairs to the room Ryan is even more surprised than before. Walking through the hall he sees multiple people having sex with each other. Sex swings, whips, chains, threesomes, foursomes, gang bangs and orgies. Ryan whiteness one guy fucking another guy and a girl fucking that guy with a strap on. Is that the Mayor? Yes, it is. I fucked him he's a decent lay, Kathy laughs. Here's our room. Kathy opens the door to a room filled with sex toys and a big bed.

Kathy walks over to Ryan and unzips his pants. I always wanted to know what your dick looked and felt like. Ryan hates the way his dick looks on soft. On soft Ryan's penis is only 3.5 inches. Kathy starts to stroke Ryan's dick. Ryan tries to resist the urge to get hard. Ryan's dick starts to grow. Oh my, you are a grower I see, Kathy smiles. Ryan's dick springs up to full attention. You have a very nice dick. How big are you? It's 7 inches and ¾'s. Mmm, way bigger than my husbands. It's not as thick as I thought but it's really nice. Tie me up, Kathy demands Ryan. Don't try to run either the door won't open unless I want it to. Ryan agrees and straps Kathy down. Get that whip over there and I want you to whip me baby. Ryan goes and gets the whip. He gives Kathy some light lashes. Don't be a pussy whip me. Ryan filled with slight anger whips Kathy as hard as he can. Kathy starts to scream in enjoyment. Come over and fuck me she demands. I don't have a condom. I don't want you to wear one so just come on. Ryan walks over and inserts himself inside her. Mmm, it feels so good she says. Ryan starts to fuck Kathy slow. Fuck me harder. Ryan agrees, he doesn't say anything and fucks Kathy as hard as he can. Fuck I'm going to cum! Kathy screams. Ryan is happy it's almost over. Ryan looks over and there are a group of men watching and waiting at the door. They start to cheer Ryan on. Cum in her man he hears. Being watched kinda excited Ryan. Kathy's orgasm was intense she shook the whole bed. Ryan couldn't hold back anymore. Ryan pulled out of Kathy and shot his load all over her hair and face. Fuck yes! Treat me like a slut. Can we join in? The men at the door eagerly await an answer. Yes please, Ryan you can go take the car I'll be fine here. Are you sure? Yes, I know everyone here. Ryan grabs his clothes and bolts out the door. The men and Kathy continue to have a great time.

After the story Erika is shocked by Ryan's story. Wow! You got me too'd. Seems that way Ryan shakes his head. Please don't say anything. I won't, you have my word on it. Kinda curious now about this hidden sex club, Erika laughs. It's kinda weird but sexy now that I know how big your dick is, she laughs. I'm sorry, I could have left that part out. It's cool I won't tell anyone. I really think that was messed up. Ryan and Erika hugged and resumed their day.

CHAPTER 7

So we meet again

It's an 85-degree weather day and Jamel is out riding his bike. He pulls into the ice cream spot to get a root beer float. He's been riding almost all day and wants to take a little bit to relax. While standing in line Jamel feels someone grabbing near his dick. Yo! What the fuck are you doing? Jamel turns around and to his surprise it's Keisha. Well isn't this a surprise. I would have never thought I would have saw you again, Keisha has a big smile on her face. You can't just be grabbing on people, Jamel laughs. That's how people get knocked out. The only thing I want knocked out by you are my pussy walls, Keisha smiles. Oh word, do you even remember my name? Hmm, I know it's starts with a J. I'm surprised I forgot your name with that great dick you have. Wow! You can't remember my name, but you want to fuck me? What do I look like a hoe? Jamel has a straight face. I'm sorry I didn't mean to disrespect you; Keisha turns in shame. It's alright, I'm just messing around. It's Jamel, he smiles. I remember yours though Keisha, he laughs. Of course, Jamel couldn't forget the name of the woman that helped cause a rift between Karah and him and the one who fucked him good on a nude beach. Keisha smiles, what are you doing later? I'm just going to head home. Can I come over? I mean you don't know me like that, but you want to come over to my house? It's ok, I trust you. I mean I already fucked you and we didn't know each other, and I need that dick again. Alright, come by at like 11, Jamel smiles. Jamel gives Keisha his address and they exchange numbers. Jamel finishes his root beer float and heads back on his bike and starts to head home.

Jamel is at the light. He notices someone is trying to wave him down. Jamel flips up his vizor and still can't tell who is waving at him. Jamel pulls over and the car pulls over behind him. Jamel hops off the bike and takes of his helmet. He starts to walk to the car and the driver winds down the window. Hey there stranger. Oh shit! What's up Aiyana. How have you been? I've been good, Aiyana smiles. It seems like you've been ducking me. What's up with that? Jamel is curious to what happened. I'm sorry, I have a lot going on and I'm extremely busy. I get that and it's all good, Jamel smiles. So, what are you doing later? Aiyana says starring Jamel up and down. I still never got to see how big that dick was. I don't have anything planned. What are you trying to do? You didn't just get the hint of what I'm trying to do? Aiyana laughs. Hey, I need full consent and understanding. I'm not trying to get me too'd out here, Jamel laughs. Well I'm trying to fuck. I just like to be honest. Can I come by around like 11? How about you come by around 1:30. Is that cool? That's actually great. I'll text you my address, Jamel says. Ok great, Jamel walks gets back on his bike and they both pull off.

It's 11:10 at night. Jamel hasn't heard from Keisha. Jamel didn't text her because he figured if she didn't come, he still has Aiyana to fall back on. Well, I guess she's not coming, he shrugs his shoulders and continues to watch Tv. Jamel falls asleep on the couch

Jamel wakes up to a knock on the door. Oh shit! I fell asleep. He looks at his phone and it's only 11:30. He starts to laugh as he walks to the door. Hey Kei, Jamel pauses. Who's Kei? Aiyana says standing at the door. I didn't say Kei I said cutie. I just couldn't get it out because you look so beautiful. I'm confused though because I thought we were supposed to link up at 1:30. We were I just couldn't wait anymore so I finished what I had to do and thought I would surprise you. Well I'm definitely surprised, Jamel laughs. Maybe this was a mistake. I'm sorry for just showing up, Aiyana starts to walk away. Jamel grabs her hand. No, don't go. I want you to stay. You can't come over here all beautiful and just dip out on me. How are we supposed to feel? We? Aiyana looks confused. I'm talking about us me and him. Jamel points and grabs his dick. Aiyana walks through the door and sits on the couch. Jamel sits next to her. Is it alright if we just hang out for a little? Aiyana wants to feel Jamel out before she gives up her goods. Yes, that's fine with me. Jamel is alright with just hanging out it's been a while since he just hung out with a girl. Jamel puts on a comedy special and slides over next to her and places his hand around her shoulder.

Jamel is constantly looking at his phone to make sure Keisha isn't texting him. Is everything alright? Aiyana notices Jamel isn't paying attention to the special. Oh yeah, everything is great. It's not too often I get to chill with a girl at my house. Really? I must be special then, Aiyana laughs. You must be. I mean when I first met you in that car, I looked at you and felt like you could be wifey material but then. Then what? You ghosted me. It's all good though. Aiyana places her finger on Jamel's lips. Shhhh, I'm here now. Aiyana leans in and kisses Jamel softly on his lips.

Aiyana places her hand in Jamel's lap and grabs his dick. Oh my! Aiyana jumps up. What's wrong? You weren't lying you are packing. Jamel starts to laugh. Wait until it gets fully hard. Jamel moves Aiyana's hand and stands up. He walks to his bedroom. Aiyana follows right behind him. Aiyana lays on Jamel's bed with her legs spread. Jamel is only in his beater and basketball shorts. He pulls down his shorts and reveals his semi erect shaft. Oh, I see you weren't wearing any underwear, Aiyana laughs. Nah, I like to be comfortable. Jamel walks over to Aiyana and helps her undress. Aiyana stands fully naked in front of Jamel. She tries to cover her body with her hands. Let those hands down. I want to see all of that body. Aiyana slowly lets down her hand. Her 32 A breasts catch Jamel's eye. Damn! You're so beautiful. Thank you, Aiyana says with a sexy smile. Aiyana is a skinny girl who sometimes suffers from weight issues. She has a slim body type and stands about 5'0 weighing 110 pounds of pure beauty. Jamel can't take his eyes off of her nipples. Her nipple rings are shining bright. Jamel looks down and stares at Aiyana's pussy. I'm sorry, I forgot to shave. Aiyana feels slightly embarrassed. Don't feel embarrassed I love some hair on pussy. Let me taste it. Aiyana walks over to Jamel. He drops to his knees and begins to kiss her lips. Her pussy starts to moisten more. Mmm, your pussy tastes good. Jamel gets up and lays down on the bed. I want you to ride my face. Aiyana walks over and places her pussy on Jamel's face. She starts to grind while Jamel sticks his tongue out catching all her juice. Jamel holds Aiyana still and works on her clit, lightly sucking and swirling his tongue around.

I'm about to cum! Oh god! Eat my pussy! Aiyana cums all over Jamel's face leaving him drenched in her juices. Jamel stands up. His dick is rock hard from eating Aiyana's juicy pussy. Aiyana looks at Jamel's dick as it stands up at full attention. I never seen something so beautiful in my life, Aiyana says smiling. Jamel walks over to her and spreads her legs. He slowly tries to enter her but has some issues. Damn, your pussy isn't trying to let me in. Your pussy is wet as fuck so I'm not sure what's up. Well I haven't had sex. You mean you haven't had sex lately or ever? I haven't had sex at all. I'm a virgin but please don't stop I really want this to happen. Jamel is hesitant, he usually doesn't like to fuck virgins. Alright, I'll take care of you then, Jamel smiles. He bends over and starts to eat Aiyana's pussy some more. She's enjoying every second of it. Jamel gets up and tries to ease his dick in and it goes in slightly. See, we are making progress. Wait a minute though, he says as he stands up. Since it's Aiyana's first time Jamel walks over picks up his phone and turns on some music to lighten to mood. He turns on his favorite R&B sex play list. He walks out the room and comes back a few moments later with candles and a lighter. Jamel lights and places candles all over the room. The beautiful aroma starts to fill the air. Now the mood is perfect, Jamel smiles and walks back over to Aiyana. He lightly kisses Aiyana's neck. Light moans start to leave her lips. Jamel positions himself to enter her again. Aiyana's pussy is even more wet now than before. Jamel enters Aiyana slowly again. Aiyana hugs Jamel close. Jamel goes halfway in and pulls back out. He only wanted to give her half of him since it was her first time. It hurts a little, Aiyana says. It will hurt at first, but it will start to feel good soon. Aiyana looks at Jamel and smiles. Jamel continues to fuck Aiyana slow. Jamel looks at Aiyana's face and what once was pain turned into pleasure. It does feel good, she moans. Fuck my virgin pussy. This pussy is all yours, she says in enjoyment. Jamel loves shit talk. He gets overly excited and goes deep inside her. Oh fuck! Aiyana screams out. I can't take it pull out please. Oh, shit I'm sorry. Are you alright? Yes, I'm fine. Please keep going but not all the way. Jamel enters her halfway again. He strokes slowly kissing her neck. You're so beautiful, Jamel whispers in her ear. He looks at Aiyana's face and notices tears. Jamel pauses, is everything alright? Yes, don't stop. I'm just happy that's all. Jamel speeds up his strokes slightly. Aiyana clinches Jamel even tighter. Her nails dig in his back. Oh baby, I think I'm about to cum!

Jamel keeps a steady pace. I want you to cum with me, Aiyana screams out. Jamel speeds up a little more. He starts to grunt. Fuck I'm about cum too. Oh shit! They both scream. Jamel shoots his load inside Aiyana and she cums all over his dick. Jamel pulls out of her and looks at his dick covered in blood and cum. That was great, Aiyana smiles. Yes, it was, Jamel smiles back. They lay next to each other enjoying the moment.

After laying there for about 15 minutes Jamel looks at his phone. He sees a message from Keisha. Hey, I'm sorry I'm super late. I should be there soon. I know I should have let you know I was still coming but I wanted to surprise you but then thought that would be weird. Oh shit! What's wrong? Aiyana asks. Oh, nothing I just realized I have a lot to do tomorrow and need to get some sleep. So, what are you about to do? What do you mean? Aiyana looks confused. Do you need me to order you an Uber or a cab? No, it's ok I drove here. Alright cool, Jamel smiles. Aiyana gets her clothes on and walks to the door. When will I see you again? Aiyana asks. I'm sure you will see me soon. Aiyana kisses Jamel and walks out the door to her car.

Jamel leaves the candles lit. He goes to the bathroom and washes off his dick. He doesn't take a shower since he is not fully sure when Keisha will arrive. He walks in the room and takes the sheets and blanket off the bed and throws them in the washing machine. Damn, I can't believe she was a virgin. I wish she would have told me prior to me trying to fuck her. I hate taking virginities. Jamel places new sheets and blankets on the bed and waits for Keisha to arrive.

A few minutes later there is a light knock at the door. Jamel opens the door naked with nothing on. Damn! What a great view, Keisha says while starring at Jamel's big dick. Jamel moves to the side and Keisha walks in. It smells really good in here. I had to make it nice for you, Jamel says while smiling. Wow! All this for me I feel special. Jamel's dick wastes no time springing up to full attention while talking to Keisha. I see someone is especially happy I'm here, Keisha says with a big smile. Jamel wastes no time and walks Keisha back to the room. The candles are still lit from earlier. Keisha drops to her knees and grabs Jamel's rock-hard dick. So, we meet again, Keisha says while lightly kissing the tip of Jamel's dick. Keisha runs her tongue up and down Jamel's shaft then takes his dick deep in her mouth. Oh shit! Damn! This shit feels good. Just tasting Jamel's dick makes Keisha's pussy start to drip. Mmm, she says while taking Jamel's man hood deep down her throat. Jamel takes Keisha's head and starts to fuck her face. Jamel can't take his eyes off of Keisha as she makes love to his dick with her mouth. Jamel pulls his dick from her mouth and moves to the bed. Jamel lays on the bed. Keisha starts to walk over. She strips down completely naked. Damn! I love that beautiful chocolate skin; Jamel says starring at Keisha's body. I need you to come over here slow. Keisha walks over nice and slow and crawls on the bed to Jamel. She lays next to him and they kiss passionately.

15 minutes has gone by and Jamel and Keisha are still rubbing and kissing each other. I need you inside me, Keisha whispers in Jamel's ear. Jamel's rolls on top of Keisha. He kisses her neck and works his way down to her breasts. Jamel flicks his tongue and lightly sucks her nipples. Keisha reaches down and grabs Jamel's dick to position him to enter her. I said I need you inside me, Keisha says to Jamel. Jamel doesn't say anything. He starts to enter Keisha. Keisha's pussy opens up for Jamel. Keisha gasps as Jamel enters her inch by inch. He goes 8 inches deep and Keisha can barely take it. You are so big. Jamel goes an inch deeper now 9 inches of his 12-inch dick is inside Keisha. She places both hands on Jamel's ass and grips his cheeks. I'm going to cum, Keisha says moaning. She holds Jamel tight and cums all over Jamel's dick.

Jamel and Keisha have been having sex for close to 45 minutes. Keisha is amazed at Jamel's stamina. Fucking Aiyana before Keisha came is helping Jamel not bust. He tends to last way longer when he gets his first nut off.

Jamel hasn't been taking as much during this session with Keisha. He's been focused on fucking the shit out of her. Keisha looks in Jamel's eyes. This is the best dick I ever had; Keisha says moaning. Are you ready to take all of it? Jamel still has only gave her 9 inches of his dick. I don't know if my pussy can take it. We've been fucking for almost an hour and you still haven't even been close to cumming yet. Don't worry about me. This is all about you, Jamel says with a smile.

I want it to be about you too, Keisha smiles back. Plus, I'm not sure if I can take to much more of you. Your dick is way too good and big to be fucking all night. You aren't on any drugs, are you? Drugs? Hell no, Jamel says with a straight face. I just got some bomb ass dick. Yes, you do Keisha laughs. I didn't give you all of it you still had about 3 inches to go, Jamel laughs. I don't know if it was better this time or at the beach. I would say the beach. Why is my pussy trash this time? No, it's just the experience was way different. I have never been to a nude beach and I never fucked a random girl on one. That shit was fantastic. Oh, alright I was about to say if my pussy was trash that's a heart breaker. If your pussy was trash, I definitely would tell you, Jamel laughs. Well, that is good to know. We need to do this more often if that's alright with you, Keisha says looking away to avoid eye contact just in case Jamel declines. I'm down for that, Jamel says with excitement. I def can't wait to make you feel every last inch. I can't wait either, Keisha says with a huge smile. So, I was wondering if you would be busy next Friday night. I'm sure I don't have anything to do. Why? What's up. Well, my friends and coworkers are having a get together and I always usually go alone, and they are usually there with their partners. So, I was wondering if you would like to go with me. Jamel pauses before he answers. I know we don't really know each other so I completely understand if you don't want to go. Jamel smiles, of course I would go with you. Even though we don't know each other that well I wouldn't mind getting to know you more. How do you want to meet up? Should I meet you there or what? I can pick you up it would be nice if we came in together. Are there any rules I should know beforehand? Jamel is curious because he doesn't want to disrespect anyone's home. No, there isn't. My friend who usually has it has a lot of money, so their house is pretty big. She can sometimes come off as a snob or rude. She has worked for everything she has so I'm not trying to disrespect her, but I feel sometimes she forgets where she came from. I understand, I won't let that bother me or anything, Jamel smiles.

Jamel and Keisha lay there together until they fall asleep in each other's arms. Even though they barely now each other Jamel feels a strong connection with Keisha. A feeling he hasn't felt in a long time.

It's later in the afternoon and Jamel wakes up before Keisha. He goes to start the shower. Good morning, he hears from behind him. Damn girl! You're like a cat I just looked over and you were still sleep. I always have to be light on my feet, Keisha laughs. I see, says laughing too. I hope I didn't overstep staying her last night. Nah, it's all good. I didn't mind at all. Only thing that's bothering me right now is that morning breath. Oh my god! I'm so sorry. It's all good, Jamel bursts out laughing. I'm just playing with you. I always keep extra toothbrushes. Jamel opens the drawer and picks out a toothbrush for Keisha. Thank you, Keisha smiles. You're welcome, Jamel smiles back. Can I get in the shower with you? Of course, you don't have to ask me to get in the shower with me just hop on in.
Before we get in, I need to do something, Keisha says with a smile. Keisha drops to her knees. I need you to bust in my mouth. I never got a chance to feel or taste your cum last night. Jamel takes his dick and smacks it on her lips. Well make sure you swallow all of my nut. I want it in my mouth and on my face. Keisha holds Jamel's limp dick in her hand. Keisha starts to suck on his shaft. Jamel's dick is stiffening in her mouth. Mmm, I can still taste my cum on you, Keisha moans. Tell me how it tastes, Jamel says with a smile. It tastes so good baby. Keisha stops talking and takes Jamel deep in her throat. She holds Jamel's dick in her throat for as long as she can then releases. Keisha does that over and over again. Fuck! I swear you give some of the best head I have ever gotten, Jamel screams. Keisha takes her hands and jerks Jamel's dick while she is sucking. She light sucks the tip then goes back deep again. Turn around Keisha demands. Jamel turns around not sure what's about to happen. Keisha spreads his ass checks and eats Jamel's ass while stroking his dick from the back. Oh shit! I want you to cum for me baby, Keisha says in a sexy voice. Fuck! I'm about to cum! Jamel dick tightens and he shoots his load. Keisha catches it with her hand and proceeds to rub it on her face and liking it off her fingers. Mmm, I love milking you, Keisha smiles and they hop in the shower.
After a 45-minute shower they get out and get dressed. I can't wait to see you again, Keisha smiles as she heads to the door. I can't wait either, Jamel's smiles. Jamel goes in for a hug but is met with a juicy kiss. Keisha walks out the door hops in her car and heads home. Jamel decided to go back to sleep for a little. Damn, I love my life, he says laughing and lays down.

CHAPTER 8

Good Friends

It's 12 in the afternoon and Jamel is getting dressed to start his day. There is a light knock at the door. Jamel is naked so he walks to the door and cracks it open to see who it is. Boy, let me in! A woman's voice barks as the door is being pushed open. Jamel recognizes the voice instantly. In walks a beautiful West Indian girl Devyani. Wait! I'm naked. Like I haven't seen that dick before. Yeah true, Jamel laughs. So, what's up Devy? Nothing much I just wanted to stop by and see how you were doing. As you can see not much. Jamel walks to the back room and puts some boxer briefs and a shirt on. I miss you man. You don't check on me all that much anymore, Jamel says starring at her. Devyani and Jamel have been friends since high school. They didn't like each other at first but became really close as they got older. I know I'm sorry, I need to get better at communication, Devyani laughs. Plus, I wanted to show you these. Devyani lifts up her shirt and her 36D breasts fall out of her bra. You have some pretty titties. I see you got your nipples pierced it looks good. Thanks, Devyani smiles. Devyani is a very nice girl and one of Jamel's best friends. They have never had sex or attempted and sexual relationships. Devyani stands 5'2 she has an average body build with long black hair, brown skin, a pretty smile and bubbly and goofy personality. Jamel often said he thought they would make a great couple and Devyani would say it wouldn't have worked because she would drive him crazy, but Jamel always counters with he would be one of the only ones who could take her crazy.

Yo, speaking of nipple rings. You won't believe what happened to me the other day. What girls head have you fucked up now? Devyani laughs. Man, it wasn't even like that. Remember that girl I was telling you about? Which one? You mess with so many girls sometimes I think your dick is going to fall off, Devyani starts to laugh. Man whatever, I'm talking about Aiyana. The middle eastern girl. Oh, I remember she's the one that ghosted you right? Yes, but the other day we fucked. Really? How was it? It was alright. When we were about to fuck, she hit me with a bomb. Devyani sits up in the chair. What bomb? She told me she was a virgin. Devyani's face is in shock. Whoa! I hope you didn't just fuck her and dip on her. Man, she turned out to be bat shit crazy. I had no choice. That's really messed up Jamel you shouldn't do that. You are really going to play around with the wrong girl and end up in a bad situation. I feel like I already am, Jamel sighs. What makes you say that? Jamel pulls out his phone and strolls through his text messages. It hasn't been that long since we fucked, and this woman sent me 200 text messages. Wow! 200? What do they say? The first one was Hey baby. I didn't respond, then she texts me 20 minutes later hey stranger, then a few messages she sent me love gifs and heart eye emojis. The last message she sent said "I can't believe you would fuck me and ditch me. You dirty dick bitch. You're a loser who doesn't have anything going for his self fuck you I'm done I can't believe I fell in love with you." She is really hurt Jamel. Nah, she is just crazy. Who the fuck says they love someone they barely even know? I understand Jamel but you took her virginity that is sacred to some women. I think my dick is just too powerful, Jamel starts to laugh. Yeah, maybe we should castrate you? You got jokes; Jamel starts to laugh.

What's up with you though? Jamel looks puzzled by the question. What do you mean Devy? Why do you feel the need to play these women? I don't feel a need at all. I don't really believe I'm playing them. I can't help that they get attached and I'm not feeling them. That's not my fault. I tell most of these girls straight up what it is and if they don't like it, they can leave. Some of them lie like they do like it and end up with hurt feeling like it's my fault. With Aiyana I really did like her but I'm not feeling her anymore. What about the Karah girl? Well you know she had a man and shit. When we were in Jamaica her man showed up and proposed to her. She said yes and all that. We had a big fight because I ended up fucking this girl who turned out to be her friend. What! You fucked her friend? You are foul. It wasn't even like that I didn't even know and let's be honest she's fucking me and has a man so who's really the foul one? I see your point but come on Jamel. You know better. Did her man catch you? No, it's funny because she invited me to her friend's house to hang out. Are you going to go? Yes, I'm going I like her a lot and she is a really good girl. Good, then don't let her down Jamel. I won't or I'm going to try my best not to.

Devyani and Jamel have been chilling together all day. Devyani is the only woman that Jamel can spend the whole day with just hanging out and no sex being involved. I forgot how's your son doing? He's doing good, Devyani smiles. I'm surprised we have been friends this whole time and you barely see him. I know it's crazy. I feel like a terrible friend because I barely even know him. It's alright you are a terrible friend, Devyani laughs. I still love you though. You got jokes but I love you back. How's everything going with his dad? It's hell! He is such a fucking asshole. Well, I told you not to mess with him, but you didn't listen to me. I know I was stupid, but I got something great out of it. That is true you got your son. I didn't even tell you but last week his new girlfriend tried to run me over with her car. What the fuck! Why? She's fucking crazy that's why. What did he do? He didn't do anything but laugh and take her side. Damn, why do you fuck with niggas like that? I don't know. I just find them, I guess. Yo, your pussy is like a magnet for ain't shit niggas, Jamel bursts out laughing. It must be. It's also good as fuck and gets these dudes hooked. Nah, that pussy is cursed. What the fuck ever. It's a gift from heaven. Hey man, even the devil was an angel once, Jamel can't hold in his laughter. Look Devy, you're a very beautiful girl and you're smart and loving I'm sure you will find some one that is perfect for you in this world. I hope so because if not we are getting and you will be stuck with me for the rest of your life. I'm already stuck with your punk ass. That's true I'll be around forever.

Yo, so remember earlier when I was telling you about the girl who invited me to her friend's house? Yes, I remember. Well, I actually met her before. Really? Where did you meet her? Well, it must be fate or some shit because when we were in Jamaica, I met her randomly and we fucked the first day on the beach. What? Is she stalking you? Devyani has a concerned look on her face. Nah, it just so happened we ran into each other the other day. She came over and of course I gave her this A plus dick. Also, it was right after I fucked Aiyana. Really? You fucked both of them right after the other? Yes, I did. It wasn't supposed to be like this, but I was bad at planning. You are disgusting. Did you at least wash your dick? To be honest I can't remember, Jamel starts to laugh. I meant what I said earlier your dick is definitely going to fall off. Chill man don't put that out in the universe. You are on a new level of ain't shit. Well, in my defense once gain I didn't know they were friends. Karah also made it perfectly clear we were nothing to each other and I was just dick to her. Still though Jamel. There is a level of respect that you should have, and you just totally shit all over it. Yeah, we got into a huge argument and she kicked me out the room. I bet she did. You deserved it. I almost got beat up by the police and probably could have ended up dead. Wow! That is some really crazy shit. Yeah but it's all good I'm still alive and that's the most important thing.

Throughout the day Devyani has been looking at her phone nonstop. This time her face is in shock. What's up with you Devy? Nothing I'm fine. Your face doesn't look like you're fine. It's nothing don't worry about it. Oh, so now we keep secrets from each other. It's not that it's just I don't want you to freak out. I won't freak out I promise. No, I think I'll just keep it to myself.

Jamel and Devyani are walking outside when a big black truck zooms by. Devyani's face lights up in fear. Yo, you have been acting weird for a minute now what the fuck is up. It's nothing Jamel I told you not to worry about it. That shit didn't look like nothing. You damn near tried to push me down when you saw that truck. Not to mention the looks you give when you check your phone. Leave it alone Jamel. I already told you don't worry about it. How many times do I have to keep telling you? Why are you catching an attitude with me? I'm just trying to see what's up with you. First acting like you saw a ghost and now you're snapping on me like I did some shit to you. Look, I'm sorry but you know I hate when people ask me the same question me over and over Jamel. So, I'm asking because I know you're lying not because I'm being nosy. Me and you have been tight for years. Now all of a sudden you want to keep secrets. Ok bet, Jamel says shaking his head. It's not that, Devyani says trying to hold back her tears. Well, what is it then? Jamel really wants to know why his best friend is hurting.

As Devyani is about to speak the black truck pulls up quickly. A man hops out the car. I knew that was you. Are you ignoring my calls? Jamel looks confused. Yo, my man I don't know who you are but you coming off real spicy right now you need to relax, Jamel says with a straight face. Mind your fucking business! If I was talking to you, I would address you. Seeing how I'm not taking to you step to the side homie. Devyani, do you know this dude? Jamel points at the man. Bitch! Now you all quite you better tell this dumb nigga who I am. Who the are you calling a bitch? Devyani says in a fierce tone. I'm tired of your disrespect. Who the fuck do you think you're talking to? You know what happens when you get loud with me. Fuck you mean she knows what happens when she gets loud with you? Jamel approaches him in an aggressive tone. Just let it go Jamel, Devyani says to try and de-escalate the situation. I'm going to catch you later bitch. Best believe that. You're lucky I'm on papers because if not I would smack the shit out of you. I'll see you again real soon to my nigga, the man says with a smile and slight grin as he gets in his vehicle and drives off. Now I'm hungry after arguing with this dumb nigga. Let's go get some food, Jamel says rubbing his stomach.

Devyani and Jamel have been eating dinner. It's been mainly quite due to Devyani being embarrassed. Look, I can't keep eating in silence like this, Jamel says chewing his steak. I'm so sorry Jamel, Devyani says looking down. What are you sorry for? That nigga was disrespecting you. I'm not going to let anyone disrespect you when I'm around no matter who it is, Jamel says passionately. I really appreciate that Jamel, but you don't know him he's dangerous. So am I. I'm not worried about any nigga out here. You think I'm soft or something? No, I don't think you're soft at all Jamel. He is just a really really bad dude. He shoots people and all that. Man, I'm not worried about any nigga. Fuck him and his guns I can get strapped too if it comes to that. Devyani rolls her eyes. Now you know damn well you aren't about to shoot anyone. That's not you. The only thing you better strap is that nasty dick, Devyani laughs. Only one of us had an STD at this table though Devy, Jamel starts to laugh. Fuck you Jamel! I told you that in confidence and it wasn't my fault. The guy I was fucking just happened to be a hoe. So Devy, how often do you get that not so fresh feeling? Jamel burst out laughing. Nah but for real though be really careful Jamel. I will, Jamel says with a smile.

A few hours have past and Devyani and Jamel are heading out the door to leave when a familiar face stops them. Oh, I see you are out here just chilling with other bitches huh? That's real cool Jamel. So, you can't hit me back, but you can be out here with all these other girls. I knew I shouldn't have messed with you. Jamel, who is this girl? Devyani is confused to the situation. Bitch! Don't ask my man shit! If you don't know me, you are about to. First of all, I don't know who you are calling a bitch. Second, if you were his girl you must not be that damn important because I never heard of you. You must be one of the throw aways that Jamel has, Devyani says laughing. Alright chill, Jamel says to calm the situation. First thing, you are not my girl. You need to stop with this bullshit. Devy this is the girl I was telling you about. Oh, so this is the crazy virgin. Now it all makes sense. Girl, he doesn't want you so I think you should go on about your business. Wow! You really told this bitch our business? I knew you were a piece of shit, but I didn't think you were that low to run your mouth. You may have a big dick, but you definitely have female tendencies, Aiyana says in a sarcastic tone. Bitch! Ain't nothing female about me. You got me fucked up! Jamel backs Aiyana into the wall in an aggressive manner. Aiyana balls up her fist and swings with all her might at Jamel. Jamel barely dodges the punch almost hitting him in the eye. Jamel grabs Aiyana by the arms and pushes her against the wall. Bitch! I will fuck you up! Don't you ever swing at me again! Jamel is in a rage. He can barely control his temper. Aiyana stands there frozen. Did you just put your hands on me? You put your hands on the wrong one. You will regret ever touching me, Aiyana says in a light but serious tone. What the fuck are you going to do? You can't do shit to me bitch! Jamel really wants to put hands on her but his mental image of his mother pops into his head and he eases up on his grip and anger. Devyani places her hands-on Jamel's chest. She looks at Aiyana with a bit of sadness. Please just go we don't want anything else to escalate, Devyani says with a soft concerned tone. Aiyana stares Jamel up and down and walks away. Jamel, I think you really need to be careful with her. I don't think this is the last you will see if her. She looked serious and I feel she may try and do something crazy. I think maybe you should call the police or file a report, Devyani says I'm a soft tone. Police report? I'm not going to any fucking police. What the fuck do I look like? I'm no soft as bitch and I'm not scared of that bitch either. What can she do to me really? She isn't going to do shit and I don't have to worry about shit, Jamel says with passion. Look, I hear you Jamel, but you need to understand that she is not mentally well. You may think you have this all figured out, but you will definitely see that you don't if you don't take this seriously. It's not a game and she should not be taken lightly. I've seen women like her before she can ruin your life. You really did a number on her and I feel like you are just acting like it's no big deal. Devyani is trying hard to reason to Jamel. Jamel turns his head away and sucks his teeth. I told you already I got this. Why do you keep going on and on about it? I'm not scared of that bitch she will get over it just like all the other ones do. Did you see her Jamel? She will not because she is hurt. I know that look and that look is revenge, that look is pain, that look is heartbreak, that look is a look of a disrespected women. Devyani tries to plead with Jamel to make sure he understands the situation. One day you will see Jamel that all women are not meant to be played with and seems like she will be the one to show you. You don't want to hear this, but your past will catch up to you and you better hope that god is on your side because you just unlocked the devil, Devyani says with a serious look on her face. Man, whatever like I said, I'm not about to worry about that bitch! You are supposed to be on my side Devy not hers. I'm your friend. You are supposed to have my back, Jamel says touching Devyani's shoulder. No Jamel, I'm on the side of right and wrong and yes you are my friend my best friend at that but as your friend I have to tell you when you're wrong and you are dead wrong. Being a good friend is about honesty and honestly you are a trash ass nigga when it comes to women. I'm only telling you because I love you. I want you to be better and I want you to be the best you can be just like you want from me. I get that Devy but come on let's be real what can she possibly do to me? Devyani looks up at Jamel and lets out a big sigh. You know that old saying our parents and grandparents used to say "a hard head will make a soft ass" I feel you will learn the hard way Jamel and once again I hope it's not too late. Ok, whatever you say Devy. Are you ready to go because I'm tired to being here. Yes, Jamel I am ready to go. Are you staying with me tonight or are you going back home? Given all that has happened tonight I probably would be more comfortable if you just stayed at me house instead of going back home because that dude seems crazy, Jamel says with a concerned look on his face. It's alright I'm a big girl and I can handle myself so you can just take me home, Devyani says looking out the window. It's a quite ride to Devyani's house. After about a 20-minute ride Jamel pulls up to the curb. Devyani opens the door to get out but before she can Jamel grabs her by the shoulder. You make sure you call me if you need me alright, Jamel says with a soft tone. I will, Devyani says with a smile. Devyani walks into her door and Jamel pulls off.

Jamel has been home for a while but to his surprise there is a knock at the door. Who is it? There is just silence and no response. Then another knock at the door. Man, I said who the fuck is it? Jamel has some aggression in his voice. He walks over to the door and swings it open. Aww, hell no! What the fuck are you doing here Aiyana? Listen Jamel, I came here as a woman to apologize. I'm sorry for the way I acted and have been acting. It's just something new for me and I should have never lashed out on you like that. Aiyana starts to cry, and tears roll down her face. I was raised better than that and hope you will please forgive me Aiyana, says in a soft tone. I should have never put my hands on you and I'm sorry, Jamel says in a compassionate tone. It's ok just don't put your hands on me again, Aiyana says with a smile. I won't I promise, Jamel says with a smile. Aiyana gets closer to Jamel she reaches in and kisses Jamel on the lips. He's hesitant after what just happened but can't resist Aiyana's good pussy. He pulls her inside. Aiyana looks up at him. I want you to be rough with me and treat me like the bitch I have been to you, Aiyana says with a sexy tone. Oh, I got you, Jamel says with a smile. Jamel strips Aiyana down and throws her on the floor on her back. I want you to choke me. Jamel quickly gets undressed with his big dick in his hand he slides it in Aiyana's wet pussy.

I said treat me like a bitch choke me, she says aggressively. Jamel reaches up and chokes her. How's that you fucking bitch? Aiyana is silent then with a breath she says smack me. Jamel puts his hand up and smacks Aiyana in the face with a good amount of force. Take that shit bitch! Fuck me harder, Aiyana screams out. I want you deeper in me. Jamel goes deeper and deeper in Aiyana. Oh fuck! It feels so good daddy. I'm going to cum all over your big fat dick, she yells out. Aiyana's body starts to shake. The feeling from her orgasm spreads all through her body. Look you creamed all on my dick, Jamel says with a smile. I want your cum please daddy. I want you to cum in this pussy, Aiyana begs Jamel for his seed. I got a better idea. Get on your knees slut, Jamel says with force. Aiyana quickly gets on her knees for Jamel. Jamel takes his dick and smacks Aiyana in the face. His pre cum is dripping from her chin. Open your mouth, Jamel orders Aiyana. Aiyana opens her mouth wide. Jamel takes and shoves his dick down her throat. He fucks Aiyana's throat harder and deep. I can't breath Aiyana tries to yell out. Shut up bitch! Jamel screams. Aiyana lets out a small smile while tears start running down her face. Fuck! I'm about to cum! After a few strokes and the intensity it causes Jamel to bust inside of her throat letting out streams of cum. Aiyana doesn't hesitate to let his seed ooze down her throat. She doesn't waste a drop. Mmmm, my stomach is full, Aiyana says with a smile. After 5 minutes on the floor Jamel and Aiyana go into the bed and go to sleep. He wakes up in the middle of the night and hears the waters running and assumes Aiyana is in the bathroom and goes back to sleep. Jamel wakes up in the morning to see Aiyana laying right beside him. Jamel taps on her on the shoulder. Hey Aiyana, Jamel says in a soft tone. Aiyana doesn't respond and stays sleeping. Yo Aiyana, Jamel says a little louder. Yes Jamel, Aiyana says in a soft tone. Look you have to go, Jamel says in a stern tone. Why Jamel? I thought everything was fine with us? I mean we alright and I let you sleep here but shit doesn't change that we are not together and it's time for you to head out I don't know if you need me to call you an Uber or if you drove but you have to go. Wow! I thought I would give you one last chance to change Jamel but I see you will have to learn another way. Are you threatening me again? Jamel says with base in his voice. Get your shit and get out Jamel grabs Aiyana by the arm and pulls her to the door. You said last night you wouldn't do that again Jamel. A tear comes down from Aiyana's face. I'll leave but remember you always get what you put out and karma is a bitch. Aiyana gets dressed and leaves out the door. Jamel lays back down to enjoy his sleep cuddling up with his pillow and blanket.

CHAPTER 9

You Fucked up

It's finally the day of the party and Jamel is really excited. It has been a minute since he talked to Keisha, so he decides to call her. The phone rings once and a person picks up. Who the fuck is this? There is a male voice on the other line. This is Jamel! Who the fuck is this? Yo, I don't know a Jamel you must have the wrong number homie. Jamel goes through his contacts and pulls up Keisha's number to make sure he has the right one. Nah, I got the right number. Stop playing and put Keisha on the phone. Fuck you Nigga! The phone hangs up. Jamel calls back and the phone is sent straight to voicemail. Jamel calls back three more times and still the same thing. I'm going to call this shit back one more time and if this girl doesn't' answer fuck her. I should have known this bitch had mad niggas. Jamel's phone starts to ring. He looks down and it's Keisha's number calling him back. Aye, look here you bitch ass nigga. Don't call this phone again or we are going to have problems. Shit isn't sweet over here I will fuck you up. Wow, I didn't know it was like that Jamel. I'm sorry I guess I won't ever call you again. I'm not into violent men I thought you were different, but I can't do any type of domestic situation. Hold up Keisha, it's not even like that. You got some man on the phone is that your nigga or something? My nigga? No Jamel, that is my brother. He plays too much and I'm sorry for that. It's all good. Don't worry about it I was a little in my feelings when I thought you had a man, Jamel laughs. Awww, you were in your feelings. You poor baby. Don't poor baby me girl, Jamel starts to laugh. So, are we still good for tonight? Yes, we are still good, Jamel replies. Keisha face lights up with excitement. Oh, my god I can't wait until you meet my friends. I'm sure they will like you. I'm going to be honest with you Keisha. I don't really care to impress friends that much. Really, as long as you rock with me and I rock with you then that's what all really matter to me. I understand you feeling that way Jamel but I'm the type that my friends and family must get along with the person I will be dating and if they don't, I don't know if I can see myself with them in the future. Why Keisha? A friend or family member can't feel what you can for a person. They dam sure aren't fucking them unless you are into that type of stuff, Jamel laughs. Boy bye, I'm not letting any of my friends or family get any of that big ass dick and if they did, I would be pissed. That dick is only for me. I'm not going to lie Jamel I told my friend Karah how good the dick was and good thing she is married because if she wasn't, she probably would have jumped on you after I told her. Well shit she may have already tried, Jamel laughs. Yeah, whatever nigga. You just keep that Diamond dick to yourself and away from my close ones and if you ever fuck any of them you better tell me because I don't want to be out here looking stupid. I treat my friends like my sisters and brothers so don't ever play me. Jamel pauses, well Keisha, I don't want to ever play you I want us to be as straight forward with each other as possible. So, with that being said I guess I should tell you that. Hold one-minute Jamel someone else is calling. It's my friend she's calling about her party tonight. I know you were saying something but I'm sure it can wait. I'm really excited about seeing you tonight and I'm sure my friends will love you. I'm sure you were about to bring up how nervous you are, but you will do great just be yourself and I'm sure they will see a great person like I do. That's not what I was going to bring up Keisha. I told you I don't really care about their feelings, but I do care about yours. Well Jamel, If it's something that will get me upset before this party just keep it to yourself I want to have a good time I completely understand it's not really that important anyway we can discuss it another time I will see you tonight and I will try my hardest to make the best impression on your friends that I can for you, Jamel says with a smile on his face. Thank you, Jamel, I will see you later bye big dick king, Keisha laughs and hangs up the phone. See lord I try my best, Jamel says while looking up at the sky.

A few hours have gone by since Jamel got off the phone with Keisha. He is in his room when he hears and bang at the door. Open the fucking door! I know you are in there he hears the voice scream. Who the fuck is it? Jamel screams back. It's the police open the fucking door, or we will kick this bitch in. Man, stop playing at my door who the fuck is it? I'm not going to tell you again the man screams back through the door. Jamel walks to the door he cracks it a little to see if it really is the police. Oh shit, I thought you were playing. You must have the wrong house. Jamel tries to shut the door. The cop pushes the door open and makes his way inside. Yo, you can't just walk in here. I can do whatever the fuck I want, the officer says in an aggressive manner. You think you can just put hands on women huh? The cop asks. What the fuck are you talking about? Jamel is confused to what is going on. Put your hands behind your back you're under arrest. I'm not going any fucking where unless you tell me what the hell I'm going to jail for. You black bastards must not hear that well. I said put your hands behind your back. I'm about to call my attorney, Jamel says. Jamel reaches in his pocket to get his phone. Don't move your fucking hands, the officer shouts. Jamel slowly pulls his hands out of his pockets. While pulling his hands up he turns on the video to his phone. The officer walks behind Jamel and forcibly puts his hands behind his back. You niggers think you are hot shit, don't you? You dumb coons don't know how to keep your hands to yourself. Man, I ain't no fucking nigger. I'm being arrested for no reason. Of course, you didn't. You niggers love to use that excuse. Fucking porch monkey! I should break your teeth right now! I think I'm going to have a little fun with you first. The cop walks Jamel down the stairs and puts him in the back of the squad car. We have special places we take pieces of shit like you. Look if you're going to take me to jail just take me. I don't have time to hear this shit. Oh, you will be going to jail but that is not what I was talking about. You will feel pain before you go to jail. I'm going to show you what abuse really looks like boy. You don't have to do this man, Jamel says in fear. What is your name sir? Can I at least know your name? My name? The officer starts to laugh. You still haven't figured it out yet huh? I'm officer Stone. Officer stone look I don't know who I hurt in your family, but I don't know any people named stone. I'm related to the Abadi family. The Abadi family? Jamel looks puzzled. Yes, Aiyana is my sister. Your sister? How is that possible you're white. Blood means nothing when it comes to family. Her mother and father took me in and raised me when I was young. They fed me, clothed me, made sure I had a family and you have the nerve to put your hands on my family and the love of my life. I can't believe she even let a dirty monkey like you enter her. You didn't deserve to fuck her. I should have been the one to take her virginity. I should be the one who she should be having a baby with. All this should be me, but no she just had to lay down with you. Aye man, I don't know what she told you, but trust me she is not stable. She isn't even pregnant. I need you to understand I never have or would hurt her. We had our ups and downs but it wasn't anything to hurt her or me over. I saw the pictures Jamel. You can't weasel your way out of this one. Pictures? What pictures? Jamel looks confused. Officer stone pulls up to a stop sign. He reaches and pulls out his phone. Look what you did to her! Officer Stone puts his phone in the air showing the pictures of Aiyana. Aiyana's face is covered in blood, her cheeks are swollen, and her body covered in bruises. Yo, this bitch is trying to set me up. I didn't do that shit man. Jamel is pleading with officer Stone. Bitch? You have the nerve to call her a bitch. Oh yeah, I'm definitely going to enjoy this. Officer stone pulls into an abandoned building. He opens the door and pushes Jamel on the ground.

Back on the other side of town Keisha has pulled up to the party. I'm so excited, she says getting out of the car. Keisha walks up to the door. She knocks once, opens the door and walks in. Hey, I'm here she yells. We are all in the kitchen, she hears. Keisha walks to the kitchen where she is met by five women and six men. Wow! it's been a long time since we all have been here together Keisha smiles. Sitting around the table is Alexis and her husband Malik, Destiny and her boyfriend Xavier, Jada and her husband Jeremiah, Tiana and her husband Eli, Trinity and her boyfriend Chris, and Cam. I see you came here alone. What you couldn't find a man to come with you? Cam says with a rude tone. See this is why no one likes you Cam. You always talking shit. Plus, I don't see anyone here with you, Keisha says in a smart tone back. I'm surprised you are here anyway and not under some bathroom stall sucking STD dicks. See now you took it to far I was just playing with your stupid ass, but you just had to take it there. Damn son, why did y'all even invite this nigga? Xavier says shaking his head. Cam looks over at Xavier and gives him a death stare causing Xavier to look away. Destiny jumps in both of you need to quit it. We all came here to have fun and a good time. Not to fight and argue. Besides I heard that Keisha is getting some good dick lately, Destiny says laughing. She isn't the only one, Cam says laughing too. What are y'all down here talking about? Karah says walking into the kitchen. Oh nothing, we were just about to hear about Keisha getting some new dick, Jada says smiling. Baby, we don't want to hear that shit! Jeremiah says with a stern tone. I'm sorry daddy, Jada says smiling. Karah, how the hell are you late to your own get together at your own house? Alexis says laughing. I'm sorry, I was upstairs and heard the arguing. So, I said let me hurry up and come down here and see what's going on. It was nothing just Cam being messy, Trinity laughs. Where is Ryan? Eli asks. He is still upstairs. He was sleeping. Oh, you put that good pussy on him huh? Cam says laughing. No, I didn't he was just tired he should be down in a little while. Until then I think we should start off by playing a game. I was thinking about the classic never have I ever. The rules are simple if you have done the thing the person has not you take a shot. The one who takes the most shots loses. Ryan walks into the kitchen. What did I miss? Nothing yet we are just getting ready to play a game. Oh, really what game? Never have I ever, Karah smiles. This should get fun, Ryan laughs. I'll get the shot glasses. Is everyone drinking light or are we going dark? Let's go light. Do you remember what happened last time we went dark? We almost ended our friendship, Trinity laughs. Yeah, you are right, Ryan smiles. Ryan brings out the shot glasses along with 2 bottles of Ciroc and one bottle of Patron. Alright, it's time we get started who wants to go first? I'll go first, Destiny says. Um, never have I ever fucked someone I just met. Keisha, Eli, Malik, Jada, and Cam take a shot. Chris it's your turn. Ok bet, never have I ever been in an orgy. Well damn, Cam says. Why did you say damn Cam? Ryan asks. One by one the ladies pick up their shit glasses and take a shot. Malik picks up his glass and takes a shot too. Eli looks around in shock. Wait, did all of you do this together? He asks. Baby it was a long time ago. We were way younger it didn't mean anything, Tiana says. It didn't mean anything? Cam laughs. So, you are going to sit here and lie in his face. Don't start Cam, Malik says with a serious tone. You are the one that fucked all of them Malik and almost caused an end of a friendship. Nigga, how the fuck did I almost end a friendship? Don't act like I wasn't there Malik. I was watching remember. You were giving way more attention to Tiana than anyone which caused Alexis to get pissed. I remember you stroking her deep with that fat dick. She could barely take it. You busted in her, got her pregnant and had to sneak and get an abortion. What the fuck Cam! Why are you saying all that everyone didn't need to know about that last part! Alexis screams. Girl don't get mad at me for only speaking the truth. Nigga! this is why once again no one likes you. You do this bitch ass shit. I can't stand faggot niggas like you, Xavier says starring at Cam. Faggot! How the fuck you going to sit here and call me that. Fuck you! You are a solid bitch. Since we releasing secrets how about we spill some of yours? I will fuck you up in here! Xavier screams. I guess that's the only thing you will be fucking since you seem to not know how to fuck Destiny. Xavier gets up and walks towards Cam. He reaches back and throws a hook. It connects hitting Cam in the jaw. Cam stumbles, he regains his composure and throws a jab hitting Xavier in his eye. That's enough! Karah screams. You will not ruin my night or my house you two need to cool off. Malik and Eli separate Cam and Xavier. I'm going to head outside and cool off. Cam walks out the backdoor. He pulls up a chair and sits to calm down. Ok, now can we please continue the game. Karah says with a sigh. Are you sure you still want to play after that? Keisha says with a surprised look on her face. Maybe we should take a little break, Ryan says in a soft tone.

I agree, Destiny says. The group separates going to different parts of the house. Keisha and Karah stay in the kitchen to talk. Keisha keeps looking at her phone with disappointment. What's wrong with you? Karah asks. Nothing I invited someone to come but I think they ghosted me. Why do you think that? Well, I have been hitting him up throughout the night and he just hasn't responded. I wonder if I scared him off, Keisha out her head down and looks sad. I doubt it. He probably got caught up into something I'm sure he will be here and if he doesn't come fuck him. I really like him though. I felt like we could build. Do you like him? or do you like his dick? Karah says laughing. Girl, both. His dick is so good and he seems like he's a great guy. I just wonder if he can stand commitment. I'm tired of just fucking I want it to be more than just sex. I want a husband and kids, Keisha smiles. Trust me having a husband isn't all that. It's nice at times but there are other times when I wish I was just single. Ryan is great but sometimes I wish he would satisfy me better. Oh, Ryan has a little dick? Keisha says surprised. No, it's not small it's medium. Definitely bigger than average. He just doesn't know how to hit my spots or make me cum. Sometimes I have to guide him. I mean there isn't anything wrong with guiding a man to show him how to help you cum Karah. I know Keisha but we have been together to long for him not to know what to do. At this point in our relationship he should be giving me orgasms left and right. We should be exploring other freaky shit. This one guy who I used to fuck with now he knew how to make me cum. His dick was big as fuck. When we first started fucking I could barely take it but as time went on I took it like a champ. We would do freaky shit and he would even suck his own dick for me. I never saw anyone do that before, Keisha says surprised. It looked so good. When he first showed me, I thought it was gay but then I thought it was sexy as fuck. Have you talked to Ryan about this? No, I haven't. I just adjust in other ways. Ryan is a great guy don't fuck it up because someone else may snatch him up. I think you just need to have a serious talk. You're right, I will soon. I'm serious Karah. He may not be perfect, but you can tell he loves you. Damn girl, you are talking like you want him or something. Should I be worried? Girl, I don't want no damn Ryan, Keisha laughs. The man I want isn't here and I wish he was.

An hour has gone past and the tensions from earlier have calmed down. Destiny and Xavier are sitting on the couch. Baby, I think it's time you went over and apologized to Cam, Destiny says in a soft voice. Why? This nigga always wants to start something but never wants to finish it. I don't know why you even like him Destiny. He is phony. He smiles in your face and does a lot of shit behind your back. You may be right, but he is still my friend and you swung on him. I know he gets under your skin but all that wasn't even necessary. I guess you are right I will go apologize. Xavier heads out the back door to speak to Cam. Yo Cam, Xavier says trying to get Cams attention. Cam looks up while sitting by the pool. Look Xavier, I don't feel like fighting anymore but if you came out here on some bull shit we can really get it poppin again. Nah, I didn't come out here for that. I came out to say I apologize. You know how I get. I get emotional and I'm still confused about a lot of shit right now. I get that Xavier but calling me a faggot was that even necessary? No, it wasn't I shouldn't have said it. So, are we good? Xavier says with a smile. No, we aren't good yet. You know what you need to do to make us good again. Man, what the fuck are you talking about? Cam looks down and makes a gesture to his dick. I'm talking about this. Cam reaches down in his pants and pull his dick out. Xavier walks over to Cam slowly. He looks around to make sure no one is around. He feels the coast is clear and reaches from behind Cam and grabs his dick. Bend over, Xavier says in a soft tone. Nah, I want you to be the one to feel like a "faggot". Get on your knees and suck my dick. Xavier looks surprised. Cam I can't, you know I only top. Nigga! This isn't an option. Get on your knees, Cam says in an aggressive tone. Cam you need to be quite I don't want everyone hearing. Boy, with this big ass house they can't hear us. Do what I said. Xavier drops quickly to his knees. He grabs Cam soft dick and places it in his mouth slowly sucking and moving his head back and forth. Cams dick instantly hardens in his mouth. Suck that shit like you mean it my nigga. Don't play with it. Xavier looks up at Cam and swallows his dick whole. That's what I'm talking about. Cam grabs the back of Xavier's head. He starts pumping hard. The pumping for Cams dick is causing spit to go everywhere. I knew you could suck some dick, Cam says smiling. Cam grabs the back of Xavier's head and fucks his throat. Xavier takes it without even taking a breath. Xavier stops and turns Cam around and pushes him back onto the chair. Take your pants all the way off and lift your legs up,

Xavier says in a soft tone. Cam does not hesitate. He quickly takes everything off and lifts his legs in the air. Xavier starts to suck Cams dick slow and deep. While sucking he sticks two fingers in Cams ass. Oh fuck! Cam lets out a loud moan. Xavier slides another finger in his ass. Damn, you know what I like nigga. Play in that booty. Cam can't hold back anymore. Fuck! I'm about to bust. Xavier starts to suck faster and harder. Cam explodes in his mouth and Xavier swallows every drop. Xavier gets up off of his knees. His dick is rock hard. I'm not done with you yet nigga. Bend over, Xavier says in a stern tone. Cam proceeds to bend over. Xavier spits on his dick and slides it into Cam. He pumps hard and fast. Yeah Nigga, take that booty. You got hard being made to suck my dick I knew you wanted this hole too. Xavier is silent. He is focused on his task. Xavier keeps pumping and pumping. Don't fight it nigga. Let that nut out Cam says. Xavier lets out a huge groan. Fuck! I'm cumming he screams. Cum in this bussy boy. Xavier shoots loads into Cams ass. His hole starts leaking. You know this is your ass. You can have it anytime you want. Just as Xavier slides out of Cam. Jamel is walking up. Yo, what the fuck! I must be at the wrong house. Xavier and Cam looked shocked. Xavier gets up quickly. Who the fuck are you? Look I got lost finding the front door to this big ass house so I hopped the gate I must have made it into the wrong backyard. Xavier stuffs his dick back in his pants. Cam pulls up his pants and underwear ready to fight. Yeah you definitely pulled up into the wrong location now you are about to get fucked up. Man look, I had a rough night. Look at my face. I got fucked up by the police and all I wanted to do is to make sure I show up to this party to make sure I didn't fake on this girl I'm fucking with. I didn't come here to fight I came to show a girl I can be there when she asks. Xavier walks closer to Jamel. I understand bro, he says with a smirk. Xavier gets within an arm's reach of Jamel and throws a punch. Jamel dodges the punch and steps back. Xavier charges at Jamel at full speed. Jamel dodges quickly. Not noticing where he is charging into Xavier falls into the pool. The sound of him hitting the water makes a loud splash. Hearing the splash Karah looks out the window. What the fuck is going on out there? Her heart stops at the sight of Jamel. In fear Ryan will see him she rushes outback. What the hell are y'all doing? Jamel looks back surprised to see Karah. What are you doing here? Jamel asks confused. Nigga, I live here. Are you stalking me? Why the fuck would I do that? You know damn well I don't move like that. Cam looks at both of them back and forth. Do y'all know each other? Cam asks with a smile. Mind your business Cam, Karah says with a mean look. Look, I must have stumbled upon this house on accident. I didn't mean to come here I thought I had the right address, but I guess I was wrong. Is it ok if I leave out the front? Hell no, hope the fucking fence like you did to come in here. Jamel shakes his hears and turns around to leave. Keisha hearing all the commotion walks to the door. Jamel? Where the fuck have you been? I have been blowing you up. Why the fuck do you look like that? You better have a good fucking excuse for being late and standing here after all this time, Keisha folds her arms and while waiting for Jamel to respond. We are waiting, Cam says placing a hand on his hip starring at Jamel. Look, I got into some shit with the police. Oh lord, this nigga done escaped from jail, Cam says waving his arms. Nah, it wasn't even like that. I just got caught up with the wrong person I wasn't on any crime shit someone is just fucking with me. I didn't mean to crash the party like this I was just trying to make it somewhere safe for real. It's alright Jamel, I am just glad you are safe, Keisha says with a smile. How about we take you in the house and get you cleaned up. Hell no! Karah screams. He can't go in there. What is the issue Karah? He has been through a lot don't be like that. Ryan is in there he can't go in there. I'm confused Karah. What does Ryan being in there have to do with us helping him? You know how Ryan is he doesn't like random people being around. Girl, are you drunk? Ryan is the most open person I know, Keisha says confused. At that moment Ryan walks to the back door. He pokes his head out of the door. Hey baby, I have to head out work is calling. What the fuck do you mean work is calling? Who the fuck has to work this late at night? Baby you know how Kathy is. When she wants something done, she doesn't care about how it impacts others. Whatever Ryan don't come back to late. Ok, I won't, and I promise I will make it up to you. Ryan leaves to go see Kathy. Look Keisha you sit and relax I will help him. I have a first aid box in my master bathroom. It's ok Karah I can take care of him. No, it's my house let me be a good host and help him out. Let's all head back inside. Xavier before you walk into my house you need to take off those wet clothes. I don't want my floors wet after I just got them done. I don't have any clothes Karah. Ryan has some fresh t shirts and shorts he never wore you can wear that. What about my draws? I can't help you with that. You may just have to let them swing, Karah starts to laugh. Everyone enters the house. Destiny looks Xavier up and down. Uh baby, what happened? Why are you all wet? I don't want to talk about it. You should have come outside like everybody else. You don't have to have such a bad attitude about it, Xavier. I was just asking. Karah pulls Jamel by his arm. You follow me, she says in a low tone. Who is that? Y'all just bringing niggas out of no where? Malik says looking at Jamel. What's up bro, i'm Jamel. I'm Keisha's guest. What's good bro. I'm Malik nice to meet you. Hi, I'm Alexis. What's up man, Jeremiah nice to meet you. Hey, I'm Jada. Karah cuts in alright let me finish it we have to get him upstairs. Those two are Tiana and Eli. The remaining two are Trinity and Chris and you met Cam and Xavier outside. It is nice to meet all of you. Jamel says with a smile. Alright, he will be back we just have to get him fixed up. Karah walks Jamel up to the 3rd floor of her house. Damn, this house is big as shit. I knew you had bread but I didn't know it was like this. A nigga could get used to this. No, a nigga like you doesn't deserve to live like this. How dare you Jamel? What the fuck are you talking about Karah? Why would you come in and be flaunted in my face like that? After all we have been through, I can't believe you would be that petty. See Karah, there you go with all the extra shit. First of all you know damn well I didn't even know where you lived. The second thing is you made it clear on multiple occasions that we would never be anything and you didn't want to have shit to do with me so why do you care all of a sudden? You know what Jamel fuck you! Fuck everything you stand for. It's niggas like you that fuck it up for the good dudes out here. Last time I checked the real person who is fucked up here is you. I bet you never told Keisha about us. I also know the real reason you didn't want me in the house is just in case your man saw me. I bet he still can't fuck you like I can Jamel says while grabbing Karah's ass. You may have a man but this and that pussy will always belong to me. Karah's pussy can't help but react to Jamel's touch. She instantly starts to get wet. Karah smacks Jamel's hand away as they reach the bathroom. You can smack my hand away, but I know your pussy just got wet. You can't get enough of this daddy dick. You are just so full of yourself Jamel. The only one of us that gets full is you every time you take this dick. Shut up and sit down on this chair boy. Damn, this is a nice bathroom. Thank you, we work hard to make sure we can maintain what we have. Karah reaches into the linen closet and grabs a first aid kit. Karah look Jamel in his eyes.

She takes the alcohol out and dabs it on a cotton ball. Karah dabs up the blood on top of Jamel's eye. Karah's anger for Jamel quickly turns into compassion. Seriously Jamel, what happened to you? Look, I'm not going to lie to you. Everything that has been preached to me came true. I fucked around with the wrong girl's emotions and I'm paying for it. A girl did this to you? Karah has a surprised look on her face. No, but she is the cause of it. She is related to this cop and told him all these lies, and the cop basically kidnapped me from my house and did this to me. Karah starring at Jamel wanted to make this into an I told you so moment but held back while seeing Jamel in pain. In a brief silence Karah and Jamel lock eyes. You still are fine as shit. I missed seeing your face. Whatever, you don't miss me Jamel. Yes, I do. There are still days when I think about you. You think about me, but you are fucking my friend. We have been over this already I didn't know she was your friend. You didn't at first but now you do Jamel and you are still here with her. I like Keisha she is a good girl. I think we would be a good fit, but you and I have something special. I know you see it just like I do. You should have left Ryan to be with me, but you didn't. Why Karah? Look Jamel, you have something that a lot of other guys don't have. At the time when we first got together, I was broken. I needed something filled and you filled me in more ways than one. So, you really only wanted me for my dick. At first yes but then it became something more. When I told you all that in Jamacia I was trying to hurt you because you hurt me. I took you on that trip and I just felt so disrespected that you fucked her, and she is one of my best friends. I know you didn't know but it still hurt. I am not good at being emotional. I don't like being hurt Jamel. I'm very selfish and I sometimes lash out on people I love. Oh, so you do love me, Jamel looks up at Karah with a smile. I honestly do and it hurts me to my core, but I know we can't go any further than we already have. I am engaged to Ryan and you and Keisha seem like you both like each other. I just hope she takes care of you because even now it's hard looking at you and not wanting to take that dick in my throat. Jamel stands up without saying a word. He reaches and grabs the back of Karah's head. With the other hand he unbuckles his pants and pulls out his dick. Karah's eyes start to light up. Jamel slowly glides her head to his long shaft. Karah opens wide and takes the tip of Jamel's dick in her mouth. She lets out a soft moan running her tongue all over his dick. I missed this big dick, Karah says with a smile. Fuck my throat. I need to feel it deep in my throat. I want to choke on this big dick daddy. Jamel shoves his shfat deep down Karah's throat. He picks up pace and proceeds to move faster and faster. Spit starts to run all down Karah's clothes. Karah takes Jamel's dick from her mouth and smacks her lips with it. She looks Jamel in the eyes. I don't care who you are with this will always be my dick. She takes Jamel deep in her mouth again. The tears start to roll down her face as she gags and coughs on Jamel's shaft. I want you to nut all over my face. Give me that nut. Jamel stops suddenly. Nah you my bitch and that is my pussy. I tell you where I'm going to cum. Bend the fuck over now! He says in an aggressive tone. Karah bends over and quickly. She doesn't hesitate to get into position. I want to feel that dick stretch this pussy. I don't plan to take it easy on you either Jamel says. I don't expect you to, Karah says back. Jamel pushes himself into Karah's wet pussy. Gaging on Jamel's dick has her dripping wet. Jamel starts to pound Karah's pussy. Oh shit! Take this pussy nigga! Yeah bitch! This is what you wanted right. Yes! Yes! Fuck me baby! Shut up bitch before my girl hears you. You like fucking this juicy pussy while your date downstairs. I want you that cum all over my ass. What the fuck did I tell you prior. I choose where I cum. The aggression Jamel is showing is sending her over the edge.Oh shit! I am about to cum all over this big dick daddy. Be a good slut and fuck this dick while my girl is downstairs. The thought of fucking Jamel while in a relationship sent Karah in a spiral. Karah's pussy clinched Jamel's dick as she exploded all over him squirting everywhere. Oh yeah, I like that shit, Jamel moans. I can't hold my shit back anymore. Cum on my ass daddy I want to feel that nut on me. Shit up bitch! I told you I cum where I want. Jamel lets out a big groan. Ah! Fuck! I'm cumming! Jamel shoots streams of cum in Karah's pussy. As he pulls out cum oozes out of Karah. Karah scoops some up in her hand and lets it drip in her mouth. They clean themselves up and head back downstairs. Everything alright? Keisha asks. Yes, baby everything is good, Jamel responds. Alright, I need you a full strength for later Keisha responds. Thank you Karah for helping take care of him. I really appreciate it. It's no problem at all I was happy to Karah smiles. Karah's pussy started to tingle. The excitement of fucking her friends man gave her a feeling she had never felt before. A couple of hours have gone by since Jamel and Karah fucked. Karah is still on the highlight of her night and can't get over what happened. Karah realizes during this time that she has not hear from Ryan since he left. She picks up her phone to text him not realizing there was a text message waiting for her. Her face turns from happiness to anger as she reads the text "Kathy we can't do this anymore". I can't believe this mother fucker! What's wrong? Keisha asks with a confused look on her face. Look at this shit! This cheating bitch! After all I do for this mother fucker and he is going to cheat on me. Keisha picks up the phone and reads the message. Maybe it's just a big misunderstanding Karah. I am sure he would not do that to you. Jamel looks over at Karah and shakes his head. Can I help you? Why the fuck are you shaking your head? No reason at all, Jamel says turning away. You know what the party is over everyone get out. Karah don't be like that towards us, Destiny says in a concerned tone. She is hurting right now, Xavier says in a calm voice. Everyone slowly leaves one by one. I'm going to call you later alright. Keisha doesn't want to leave her friend at her time of need. On the way out the Jamel grabs Keisha by the ass. He makes sure to grip it in Karah's face. Have a good night he says with a smirk. Karah is alone in disbelief.

CHAPTER 9.5

You Fucked up Part 2

On the other side of Ryan pulls up to Kathy's house. He is surprised to see another familiar car in the driveway. He walks up to the front door. The door opens and there is a man standing there with a robe. Good evening Ryan, my name is Bentley I will be your servant for the day. My servant? How did you even know my name? It is my job to know the name of the person who I am assigned to for the night. Wait, so there are more of you? Yes sir, but I am your servant for the night. Ms. Homes is expecting you. Please follow me to the changing area. Bentley walks Ryan through the home. Ryan's house was nice but compared to Kathy's it was nothing. Kathy's house was truly something out of a movie. The house was a beautiful 75-bedroom home with 40 bathrooms. The ceiling was high with a diamond in crested chandelier. The home had two pools one indoor and one outdoor. There was a sauna and a home gym. On the way to the changing room Ryan stopped to admire the indoor basketball court. Standing there he notices a young male. The young man looks over and notices Ryan and smiles. He walks over to introduce his self. Hi, I'm Kyle. You must be Ryan? Nice to meet you Kyle. How do you know Kathy? Oh, that bitch. She is my mom. Your mom? I didn't even know Kathy had kids. She likes to keep me a secret. Damn, I am sorry to hear that, Ryan says. Don't be, she usually always makes up for it by making sure I get what I want. It has been like that my whole 20 years of living. Well, it was nice to meet you Kyle. Nice to meet you too Ryan. I will see you later, Kyle smiles. Ryan has a confused look on his face but brushes it off. Ryan and Bentley arrive at his room. This is your room for the night. My room for the night? I thought this was just a changing room. Well, it is both. We can't have our guests driving late at night after the festivities. I can't stay my fiancé would kill me. Don't worry I am sure she will understand. Sir, you don't know Karah like I do. Open that top right drawer and I am sure this will help her understand. I will be back in 35 minutes to get you. Ryan walks over to the drawer. He opens the drawer and laying there is a box and a note. The note reads this is for you and the closet is for Karah. Ryan opens the box to find a diamond incrusted chain. Wow, I always wanted one of these. It looks straight out of rap video, He laughs. He walks over to the closet. Once he opens the door there are two expensive bags and a diamond bracelet. Ryan is shocked. The price tags are still on the bags one tag reads 100,000 and the other 50,000. Man, I could get used to this Ryan laughs and changes into his robe.

35 minutes go bye and Bentley is at the door waiting. Wow, you don't play. Do you? No sir, I make sure I am on time. Ryan looks down at his phone. His phone died and did not realize it. I will take care of that for you. Bentley reaches his hand out for the phone. Are you sure? Ryan asks. Yes, it is fine plus you won't be needing a phone for what is in store for you tonight. Yeah, but I have to let Karah know what's going on or where I am. Don't worry I will take care of all that for you. Alright, I am trusting you Bentley. Don't let me down. You can trust me I won't. Follow me to the bath house. The bath house? Ryan is confused due to there is a shower right next to him. Why can't I shower here? You get the full-service tonight. For our special guests we always offer the best of the best. Ryan and Bentley arrive at bath house. Man, this shit is like a house inside of a house. Well, thank you! We try to only offer the best. Would you like me to take care of you or would you like Liliana to assist? In walks Liliana. She is 5'4 light brown skin. Her long black hair falls almost to her ass. Her thick thighs catch Ryan's eye. Liliana is slim thick with a bubble that Ryan can't help but stare at. No offense Bentley but I am taking Liliana. No offense at all. Liliana this is our special guest please make sure he is taken care of. Liliana shakes her head and smiles at Bentley. Would you like massage or bath first, Liliana says. Ryan is stuck by her accent. I promise I take good care of you. Liliana smiles at Ryan. Where are you from? Ryan is curious to know her a little more. I am from Brazil. I move here 2 years ago. I work with Bentley ever since. Oh wow, do you like it here? It is alright. I miss home but it was no safe for me back there. Damn, I am sorry to hear that. It is ok. I will be fine I am strong and brave. Now come so I can help get you ready. Ryan walks over to Liliana. I will skip the massage and just take the bath. I just need a minute. You no like me? No, it's not you it's me. Ryan looks down holding his dick back from springing up. Oh no worry about that. I see all the time. I am how to you say in America down for the team. Come come, Liliana waves him over. She drops Ryan's robe and walks him over to the huge bath tub. This looks more like a pool than a tub, Ryan laughs. This water is nice and warm it feels great on my skin. What is in here? It is a mix herbs and oils such as lavender, peppermint, rosemary, jasmine, and ylang ylang. There is also Himalayan pink salt. In minutes Ryan's body starts to relax. Liliana's hands are rubbing all over Ryan's body. His dick can't help but get hard. Liliana reaches down and grabs the base of Ryan's dick.

I shouldn't be doing this. It is ok I won't tell. Liliana slowly starts to stroke Ryan's dick. It's been long time since I had dick this size. Most everyone that is invited here has small penis. I like to consider myself a part of medium meat gang, Ryan laughs. Oh no, you in gang. You be safe. Gangs are very dangerous where I am from. Oh, I am not in a real gang I was just joking around. Well enough joking and play with me, Liliana says with a smile. Ryan turns and faces Liliana. He takes her top off and exposes her nice c cup breasts. Ryan bends over and sucks Liliana's nipples. Liliana can't help but moan. Lilliana starts to kiss Ryan down his neck. She works her way down to Ryan's rock-hard shaft. Liliana immediately starts to take Ryan in her throat. Ryan is surprised how quickly she was able to swallow his dick without any warming up. Ryan stands up to get a better angle. He takes Liliana's head and presses it against his stomach. Liliana sticks her tongue out and flicks Ryan's balls. Ryan starts to fuck her throat. Faster and faster he goes. Liliana is taking it like a champ. She looks Ryan in the eyes and prepares for his load. Oh shit! I'm about to cum! Liliana pulls Ryan in locking her arms behind his legs. Ryan starts to buck. His eyes roll in the back of his head. Ryan shoots load after load deep down Liliana's throat. Liliana without hesitation swallows it all. Liliana keeps Ryan in her mouth until he starts to soften. That was amazing! That has to be top 3 best head I have ever gotten. I glad you like it Liliana says smiling. I would love to return the favor. Are you sure? A lot of people can't take what I got. Ryan is confused. What do you mean? A beautiful lady like you I would love to taste that you. Liliana waves Ryan over. Ryan walks over to her. I want you to close your eyes ok. No peaking. Ryan closes his eyes. Liliana grabs Ryan's chin. She places 3 fingers in his mouth. Ryan is surprised and confused by what is going on. Liliana reaches deep into her bikini bottoms. Out comes her 13 inch dick. She holds Ryan's mouth open and slides it in deep. Ryan's eyes widen up. He pushes Liliana off of him. What the fuck? You have a dick? Yes, they no tell you? I am trans. They didn't tell me shit. I am not into that. I like women. Bentley walks in after hearing all the commotion. I everything alright? No, why the fuck didn't you tell me Liliana had a dick. I'm sorry Ryan I didn't think it would matter. Plus, Kathy specifically requested Liliana for you. She stated you would enjoy her. What the fuck! Does Kathy think I'm gay? No, I think she feels you may be more opened minded than the rest. I don't think I am that open minded Bentley.

Everyone is opened minded for the right price Ryan. It just depends what your price is. Let me ask you this. Ryan have you ever tried it? Being with a man? Ryan says confused. No, a trans woman or well both I would say. I have not besides head. I heard you say this was some of the best oral sex you have gotten right? Yes, I did. Does it change now because she has a penis? It was still good, but I feel tricked. I'm far from being homophobic but I think taking away my choice to do something was not fair. I am sorry Ryan. I not know this was a problem. They usually send me with their favorites Liliana says looking down. It's not your fault Liliana Bentley says with a smile. We will see you later. Please follow me Ryan. I really do apologize about any confusion. Are you hungry? I can eat. What do you got? We have it all Ryan. As I stated before you are our special guest and we want you well taken care of. In that case let me get a Japanese Kobe beef steak medium with a cut of Wagyu on the side. With a side of baked macaroni and cheese and some candied yams, Ryan laughs. We never had that combo before. We knew baked macaroni and cheese and yams were your favorite, so we have that prepared. Bentley pulls out a walkie talkie. Chef Rio, can you please prepare some Kobe and Wagyu. Of course I will have that done right away. I was in the middle of preparing some for Kathy as well. Ryan is shocked. Well Ryan, looks like Kathy was thinking the same. Since it was already being prepared it will be ready in no time. Man, I must say you have made me feel like a king. The best part has yet to come you will indeed feel like a king later on. Is Kathy going to be eating with us? I'm going to guess she probably will not be. She has made it very clear she is not to see you until later on as she does not want you asking to many questions. What is so secretive that I can't find out until later? You will have to wait and see. Bentley walks Ryan down a long hallway. After a brief walk Ryan and Bentley make it to the kitchen. As they walk in, they are greeted by Chef Rio. Hello Bentley, Rio says. The food is ready please take a seat. Ryan and Bentley take a seat at the table. The table is big enough to fit at least 15 people. Ryan's eyes light up at the sight of all the food already spread out. Can I eat this? Of course, feel free to stary whenever you are ready. Ryan grabs a plate and stuffs his face. Chef Rio comes out with the rest of the meat. Eat up I hear you have event tonight for you. Damn, how comes everyone knows about tis event but me. Before you say anything, Chef Rio let me guess it's your job to know everything about the guests.

You are a very funny guy I can see why Kathy likes you. I do not work for Kathy I am her for the festivities and Kathy asked and I said I would be honored to cook for her guests. Alright I am out of here I will see you later Ryan. Chef Rio walks down the long hallway and disappears. Ryan crushes his food in no time and is stuffed. I am stuffed Bentley. This food has me tired. You are more than welcome to head back to the room for a nap. For real? I can really use one. Sure, there is more than enough time to spare. Let us head back to your room. Hey man, that is a long ass walk is there anywhere else I can sleep? I know there has to be some other room near. Well, the closest to this Kitchen is Kyles room. Would he mind? I am sure he wouldn't. Bentley and Ryan start to head to Kyles room. Out the side of his eye Ryan notices the huge outdoor pool with cabanas. Can I sleep out there? Sure, everyone loves to sleep by the pool. Ryan walks out the side door and make his way to the cabana. He splashes down on the bed there. Oh yeah, this is way nicer than being in a room. I will return in an hour and a half is that enough time for you to rest. That should be plenty. Ryan falls asleep instantly and Bentley walks away.

Only an hour has passed, and Ryan pops up from his nap. He walks back through the side door to see Bentley sitting in a chair reading. You are up earlier than expected Ryan. Yeah, I must have slept well because I feel well rested. Good because it is time for the fun to start. Follow me Ryan. Bentley leads Ryan down a long stairway to the basement. There they are greeted by a man wearing a mask. Here is your mask Mr. Bentley, the gentleman says. Thank you, you know this one is my favorite. The gentleman picks up a mask from the table and hands it to Ryan. Do not take this off unless told to do so, the man says with a stern tone. Come now Ryan we don't want to miss this. Bentley and Ryan end up at two huge doors. Bentley knocks twice and the door opens. Ryan is surprised by what he saw. Women and men completely naked with only a mask on, fountains of wine flowing, people drinking out of gold cups, the room smelling amazing like fresh picked flowers. The temperature was perfect. It was like a scene out of a Greek movie. A big horn starts to go off. Ryan starts to look around. Ryan now is the time why you find out why we brought you here, Bentley says. Bentley walks over to a throne in the middle of the room and sits down. Next to him is a woman. Ryan can tell based on the hair and body type it is Kathy. Bentley stands up to make a speech. My wife and I would like to thank you all for coming. The crowd starts to cheer. There are a lot of powerful people in this room. This is why are parties are highly sought after. We are the most secure unit I have ever saw. We allow everyone to be free and to enjoy all their kinks without the judgement of social media or unlike minded people. Our group being about secrecy and fun. It has always been our tradition for my wife and I to start things off officially. Bentley then looks at Kathy. He motions her over with his finger. Bentley whips out his dick and Kathy bends down in front of him and takes his dick in her mouth. The crowd is silent. Kathy continues to suck Bentley dry. Bentley then taps Kathy on the head to stop. Kathy pauses, for a moment. Each of us has brought a candidate to join our group. For years we have observed these prospects and trust your judgement in picking them and for those of you have been chosen if you choose to accept our invite the people in this room will take you to placed you have never been. I would like to call up my guest. Bentley looks over at Ryan. He waives him over. Ryan's face is shocked by what's going on. The crowd parts to make a way for Ryan to go through. This gentleman has been able to pleasure my queen in ways I can only imagine. He does not know but I have had a very close eye on him. I respect his ambition and his nice size cock. Even though I have not experienced it for myself. The crowd starts to laugh. Please assist me in out starting off this occasion. We shall both take my wife tonight and finish inside her to start the party. Bentley pats Kathy on the head to continue to suck his dick. Kathy arches her ass to Ryan and points to take her pussy. Ryan is nervous at first due to the amount of people. Kathy looks back at Ryan. Don't be scared this is a judge free zone, Kathy says with a smile. Kathy lines of Ryan's dick with her pussy. She slowly starts to slide him in. Ryan's nerves are instantly gone at the feel of her wet pussy. Ryan grabs Kathy's waist and starts to dig deep in her. That a boy, Bentley says cheering Ryan on. Ryan smacks Kathy's ass as he gives her all of him. Kathy moans load and the crowd starts to cheer. It is time, Bentley says standing up. He takes his dick out of Kathy's mouth and shoots his load all over her chin. Now let the party begin he says raising a glass of wine. A man walks up to Kathy and licks the cum off of her chin. His companion gets under Kathy while Ryan is still inside her. She pulls Ryan's dick out of Kathy's dripping pussy and sticks it in her mouth. She sucks Ryan's dick nice and slow. After a few sucks she takes his dick out and spits on her two fingers and rubs it on Kathy's tight asshole. Kathy starts to moan at what's about to happen next. The woman takes Ryan's dick and lines it up with Kathy's asshole. Ryan slowly starts to enter into Kathy' tight hole. I want you to fuck my ass hard. Ryan doesn't hold back. He instantly starts to pump harder and harder. That's right take my ass baby, Kathy says in between moans. I'm your dirty slut. The woman underneath Kathy is licking her juicy pussy. I'm about to cum! Kathy's body bucks as she has an orgasm all over the woman's face. The woman rubs Kathy's juice all over her face and walks away. Ryan looks around and see's all the activity going on around. Bodies on top of bodies. He feels bad for what he is doing due to Karah but feels he can't say no to Kathy due to his fear of losing his career. Kathy pulls herself off of Ryan's dick. She leans over this will be great for your career. The lady who just sucked your dick is the Mayor. The gentlemen who licked the cum off my face he is a senator. I brought you here because this is where connections can be made. If you join us, I promise you it will be worth your while. I don't know Kathy this feels like a cult. Oh Ryan, this is no cult trust me. We are just rich people who enjoy having fun in person. Y'all don't have a secret island for kids, do you? Kathy starts to laugh. No, we don't allow that in our group. Alright good, I couldn't deal with that. I have to piss. The bathroom is over there to the right Kathy points. Ryan gets up and walks through the crowd of bodies. On his way to the bathroom, he is solicited to join a few people but declines pointing to the bathroom. As he enters the bathroom, he sees two stalls one that says shit and the other says piss. Ryan enters the piss stall and notices a woman is sitting there instead on a toilet. I'm sorry I was looking for the bathroom. Oh honey, I am the bathroom. Ryan looks confused. One of my kinks which this group allows me to fulfill is I am a human toilet. The person next to me indulges in scat play so that is why there are two stalls. Do I just piss on you? How about this you piss in my mouth. I haven't had anyone to play with today everyone has not had enough alcohol yet. The woman opens her mouth wide. Ryan sticks his dick in her mouth and his stream starts to fill her mouth. The woman starts to swallow every drop. She sucks all the juice and piss from Ryan's dick. Someone was already having some fun I see she says with a smile. Yes, I was. Ryan walks out the door waiving bye the lady. As Ryan walks from the bathroom, he notices a room to his right. He peaks through the door to see Liliana and Bentley. Bentley is bent over, and Liliana is fucking Bentley deep in his ass. You know just how I like it Liliana, Bentley says. Liliana looks up and smiles at Ryan. Ryan is amazed how easy he can take Liliana's big dick up his ass. Ryan closes the door and walks away. Ryan walks and notices a thick brown skinned woman. Her ass was huge with a thin waist, her titties were big and firm. She locks eyes with Ryan. She bends over and waives Ryan over to give him the green light. Ryan walks over and the lady starts to shake her ass waiting for Ryan to penetrate her. Ryan sticks a finger in her pussy and pulls it out covered in her cream. The woman leans back and sucks his finger. Ryan starts to enter the woman slowly. Her pussy is so wet it's hard for him not to cum quick. He starts to slow stroke her. The woman quickly realizes and takes control. She arches her back and slams herself back into Ryan. You can't hold that nut with me sweetie. I like to make the men that fuck me cum quick. It's my thing. Hearing her voice Ryan starts to think. Wow, your voice sounds really familiar. The woman keeps bouncing her ass back on Ryan. As does yours. Ryan can barely hold off any longer. The mysterious woman starts to twerk on Ryan's dick. He is fighting to hold off his nut. Don't hold it honey. Bust all in this juicy pussy. Hearing the woman's voice made Ryan able to hold back his cum. I don't know if this is part of the rules, but I can't get over your voice it's like I may know you. May I have your name? I am Imani. Ryan quickly stops. He remembers the car sitting outside. Oh my god! You are not Imani Jones are you. The woman stops bouncing on Ryan. Yes, that is me she says nervously. I can't believe this. I knew I fucked up. What's wrong? She says looks puzzled. It's me Ryan Ms. Jones. Ryan! Ryan Clark? Yes, that's me. I can't believe I just fucked my soon to be mother-in-law. It's ok honey. We didn't know. I never thought you would cheat on my daughter. Though I am not surprised by what she has done to you. Ryan looks confused. What do you mean? Don't worry about that. My question is are you going to finish what you started? You want me to fuck you still? Ryan don't act like you never thought about it. I saw the way you always look at my fat ass when I come over. I know you remember the time when I stayed over because my house was being worked on and you caught me naked. Yes, I remember. I did that on purpose. I wanted you to see me. I saw how hard you got watching me while I was laying there naked. What if Karah finds out. Trust me she won't this will be our little secret. Ms. Jones slowly backs herself back on to Ryan. Cum all in your mother in laws pussy. She starts to bounce faster and faster. You know you want to. Look that my fat ass bouncing all over you dick. My daughter doesn't appreciate your dick, but I do. Let a real grown woman show you how it's done. Nut for you mother in law. Give me that cum honey. Ryan looks down at Imani's ass moving back and forth. Karah's ass was great but she didn't have shit on her mother. Oh fuck! Ryan screams. That's right give momma that nut baby. Ryan can't hold back anymore the site of Imani's ass is too much. He shoots his load deep into her. Oh yes baby I can feel that dick pulsing fill me up. I want every last drop. Imani pushes herself all the way back on Ryan milking his dick with her pussy. That was so good. I hate to say this, but your pussy may be even better than your daughters. Thank you, I am sure I had way more practice and my ass is way bigger than hers. I knew you would love it when you got it. You have been plotting on me? No Ryan, but part of me wanted to feel that dick just because. I always found the love you had for my daughter attractive and your hustle and drive would turn any woman on. It hurts my daughter doesn't see it in you, but I do. How do you think Kathy found you? I have been in this group for years. She is one of my best friends. I didn't know she would pick you to join the group but now that she has, I am excited. Horns start to go off. Bentley walks back to his throne and sits down. The time has come to see if our applicants are ready to join. The ones that did not make the cut were sent back home before we got started. I would like my guest to come up to me please. Ryan walks over to Bentley. Bentley is sitting on his throne naked. Do you accept our invitation to join our group? Ryan looks around. He makes eye contact with Imani. Who shakes her head to informing him he is making the correct decision if he says yes. Thank you for this great offer I would be honored to join. The initiation is almost complete. To join there is one thing that you must do. Ryan looks confused Bentley stands up. You must kiss my cock. I can't do that. I'm not gay. This group is about being free. Everyone that has joined had to join with doing something that was against their morals. I was like you. The group I joined prior made me get my ass fucked by a group of men. I am not into men, but I did it and now I am as successful as ever. Ryan kneels down. He puckers up and kisses the tip of Bentley's dick. Now everyone can remove their masks. The masks of the people come off. As the masks come off Karah walks through the door. Ryan! what the fuck? Ryan is surprised to hear Karah's voice. The crowd is silent. I knew something was going on. Karah looks to her left mom you are here too. What type of weird shit is going on here? Kyle walks in and stands next to Karah. Kyle what the hell are you doing? Bentley says angrily. I am just spicing up the night dad. You and mom only care about work and I am tired of this shit. You gave me Ryan's phone instead of taking care of it yourself so I thought I would invite her. The crowd starts to fade out. Don't worry everyone this will never happen again, and I promise this will not get out please everyone take your leave while I deal with this. Bentley walks over the Kyle and sticks a needle in his neck. He immediately falls out. I knew we should have left him in the hospital Bentley says to Kathy. The security takes Kyle away. Karah bolts through the door. She runs to her car gets in and speeds off. Karah is furious and is not paying attention to her speed. She is running stop signs and red lights. I can't believe this mother fucker would do this to me. All the things I have done for him. Karah loses control of the car and crashes into a light pole. She blacks out in the damaged car.

To be Continued

www.ingramcontent.com/pod-product-compliance
Lightning Source LLC
LaVergne TN
LVHW051012080826
845145LV00009B/2580

* 9 7 8 1 7 3 6 4 7 4 6 0 0 *